A Fly on the Wall

Don't think that I don't think

Keith Vire

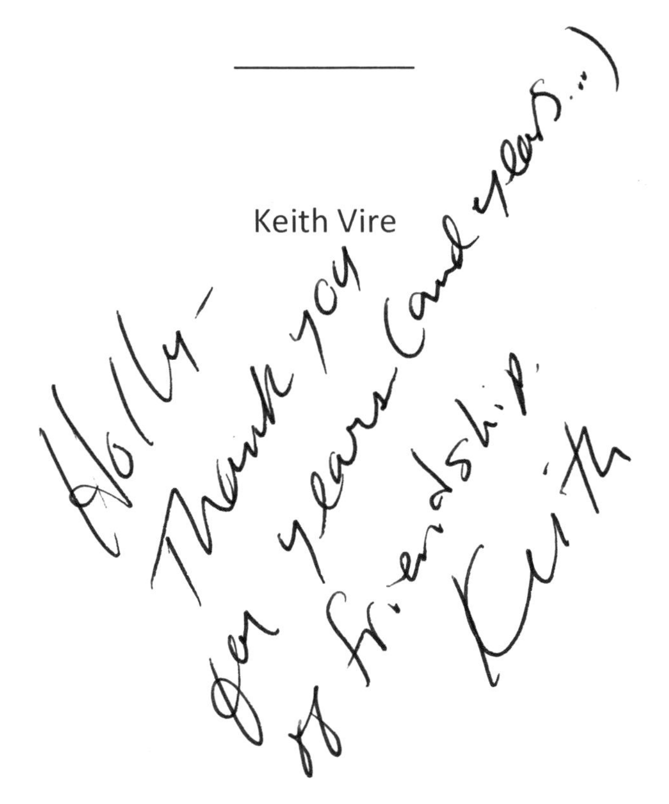

A Fly on the Wall

ISBN (978-0-615-98264-9)

Printed in USA by Keywords Press

Email: keywordspress@gmail.com

Dedication

This work is dedicated to all of the people I've known throughout my career who had way more to say than we've been willing and/or able to hear. They taught me to assume the best, to take intelligence for granted, and to never doubt that there's way more to each of us than meets the eye.

This is also for my four-year old grandson Jonah, who is clearly, in a phrase he learned well from his grandparents, THE BEST KID EVER.

Table of Contents

Preface

Analisse Brooks is certainly a real person. She isn't real in the sense that this is a biography, or a work of non-fiction, but she's real nonetheless. She was created as a tribute to the many people in my life who have autism, especially those who are considered "non-verbal" and who have faced discrimination and disrespect as a result. She is an amalgamation of all of those men and women; some of the things she says come directly from conversations that I've enjoyed with my friends throughout the years. I'm sure that my colleagues will recognize many of the phrases, thoughts, and interactions that Analisse describes, and will be reminded of a specific person, time and place.

I hope my attempt to bring a bit of education and enlightenment to the cause will be well received as well. I believe there is so much for us to learn from our friends and family members who have autism, and I tried to convey that here.

I have tried to describe Analisse and her situation in a respectful manner. I hope I have succeeded. She is real to me, and I hope she will become real to you as well.

Chapter 1:
"Don't judge a book by its cover"

My name is Analisse Brooks. My mom just calls me Anna. I'm 17 years old, and I live with my mom and go to high school. I don't know why they call it "high school". All do is sit in one room all day and color in coloring books with markers and crayons. Sometimes one of the teachers (my mom calls them para-professionals) sits with me and tries to help me do a math worksheet or something, but mostly I just sit here and do nothing. The teacher is Miss Atkins. She and the principal call this a "one to six" classroom. They write it like this: 1:6. It means that there are six students and one teacher. There are also two para-professionals here, so that's three adults for the six students we have in our room. The para-professionals are Miss Nancy and Miss Audrey. I hate that they're called Miss Nancy and Miss Audrey. If the teacher is called Miss Atkins, why don't we call them by their last names too? It makes me think we're in a day care. I don't like it because it makes me feel like everyone sees me as a child. I also don't like it because it seems like a way to separate the "real" teacher, Miss Atkins, from the not real teachers. It seems like the people who run the school want to make sure that everyone knows they're not as good as the real teacher. They even call each other Miss Nancy and Miss Audrey.

You'd think we could do some really good things with one adult for every two students, but we really don't do anything much—the three adults spend a lot of time talking to each other; about their friends, about the other teachers, about their kids, and about the students, and they think we don't understand what they're talking about. Sometimes they say really mean things, and sometimes they call us names. I watch them. I've decided that Miss Nancy is not a good person. Miss Audrey tries to do something good but Miss Atkins and Miss Nancy just look at her and make faces. They roll their eyes. Pretty soon, she stops and doesn't try any more.

None of them know that I can understand everything they're saying. I always wonder if I'm the only one.

Here's the thing about me—I have autism. Everyone thinks I can't do anything or think anything. I don't talk. I don't know why. I would if I could. I think things all the time, and I understand what's going on, but I just can't get words from where I'm thinking them to my mouth. I've decided that people must have a pipe or a tube, or maybe it's a wire or something, that connects their brains to their mouths. Words go down the tube from the brain to the mouth and come out in conversation. Something must have happened with me when I was born, and I don't have that tube or whatever it is. So, my brain works fine, but it can't send stuff to my mouth. I can make sounds, but not words, and I know that the sounds I make are part of the reason that people think I'm not smart. They're sounds that make people look at me funny. I wish I could explain why I make these sounds—I only know that I have to do it, that I can't make it stop, and I know that when I'm making the sounds, it calms me down for some reason. Inside my head, the sounds don't seem loud and obnoxious—they soothe me somehow. It's like the sound inside my head blocks out other sounds and feelings that bother me. This soothing thing is like a double problem—because the sounds make me feel calmer, I make them more and louder when I feel anxious, and I feel anxious when I'm around other people. So it's like a circle—I feel anxious, so

I make sounds; the sounds make people stare at me, and that makes my mom feel nervous; both of those things make me more anxious and that makes me make sounds. When I'm in a store or somewhere with my mom, I can see that people are looking at me—some look disgusted, some even look a little scared, and some look sad, but they all look at me. My mom is always asking me to stop, to be quieter, and I wish I could. Sometimes, people come up to my mom and ask her to make me be quiet. For some reason, this just makes it harder for me to control the sounds I make, and I get louder. It's really hard when we go to a restaurant. There are lots of people there, and there are usually lots of other noises in the room that make me anxious, so I just can't keep it quiet. Sometimes, I'm quiet in the car, and when mom parks, she'll turn to me and say, "Okay, we're going to go inside, and there will be lots of people there. Can you be really calm and quiet?" I love my mom, and I want to be quiet because I know how much she wants me to. I can tell that she's really anxious and worried about people staring, or worse, talking bad about me. We've been asked to leave lots of times, and now, we don't ever go out to eat. Sometimes, my mom goes to the drive-through at Wendy's, and we take something home, but we don't go out any more. I feel really bad about that, because I know my mom would like to get out of the house sometimes, but feeling guilt and sadness just makes it even harder for me to control my sounds.

Another weird thing about me is that I don't cry. Ever. I haven't cried since I was just a baby. My mom says that the last time she remembers hearing me cry was when I was about three years old. By that time, my mom and dad knew that something was different about me. I was missing lots of things that all of the books said that I should be able to do. My mom called them developmental stages. I was way behind other kids. I wasn't walking or talking the way I should. They took me to a specialist to have me tested. The doctor told them then about the autism. After that, my mom and dad started arguing about me all the time. My mom wanted to get help for me. My dad thought that I wasn't going to ever learn the way other people did, and he didn't think they should be wasting their time and money to try to make me "normal". He said it all the time. My mom cried a lot.

Then one day, I just stopped crying. My mom said that she didn't notice it at first. It's hard to notice something that isn't there. After a while, she started to watch closely. No matter what happened, I wouldn't cry. I didn't think my dad noticed it at the time. He just kept saying that I wasn't normal and that I was never going to be able to learn. I can remember when he said those things even though I was only three.

There's another reason that people stare at me too. The best way I can describe it is that I'm really clumsy—I guess I look weird when I walk. I don't notice it because it's how I've always been, but I hear other people talk about it. I heard Miss Nancy say that I'm spastic. I'm not really sure what that means, but I know it means that I look funny when I walk and reach for things. I've heard kids say things too—in elementary school, when my mom was still making the school let me go to classes with other kids, they would call me spaz. At first, I didn't know it was mean—I just thought I had a nickname like a lot of the kids, and I thought it meant that they were my friends. It didn't take long for me to figure out that they were just making fun of me.

I heard my mom talking with Jordan Montgomery about this once. Jordan used to be my speech therapist till my dad's insurance stopped paying. She doesn't work as a therapist now. She works at the college and helps them do research about autism, so she knows about all of the new ideas and new ways of doing things.

I divide therapists, teachers, paraprofessionals, and generally everyone that I have contact with into the good people and the bad people. I think of it like something from the Wizard of Oz—there are the good witches, and the wicked witches. Jordan is one of the good witches. Even though she isn't my therapist any more, she and my mom are good friends. That's okay. I think my mom needs a friend more than I need a therapist. She asks Jordan a lot of questions, and trusts her advice.

Jordan said that about 25% of the people who have autism have no words, or only a few. She said that there is new research that says kids who have autism and don't have speech may have motor or joint problems that are part of the reason they can't speak. Jordan reads lots of books, and she knows stuff. Jordan told my mom that 1 in 54 boys, and 1 in 252 girls are diagnosed with autism in the United States. She says that some researchers say it's increasing by at least 10% each year.

I like to listen to the experts (and the people who think they're experts) talk about autism. I learn a lot about the things I do, and the ways I think and learn. For some reason, I remember everything they say. I think not being able to talk has made me remember things more. I can remember every word of the conversations that I hear. Sometimes I hear them say things that seem really dumb to me, and sometimes I learn things that make a lot of sense. My mom is always asking questions, so I get to hear a lot of people talk about it. I wish I could talk to them sometimes, especially when they say something really crazy. Or, even better, I wish I could talk to my mom after they tell her the crazy stuff so she'd know what to believe. Once a few years ago, a chiropractor told my mom he could cure my autism if she would bring me to his office twice a week. He tried to explain to her that my condition was caused by improper alignment of my spine which caused signals from the rest of my body to get clogged up so they couldn't get to my brain. My mom talked to a lot of people before she decided this was not something she should do—she talked to Jordan, and to doctors, nurses, and other chiropractors who advised her to stay away from people who advertise anything as a "cure". They said that chiropractic medicine is a good thing for lots of people, and Jordan told her about some research that shows chiropractic adjustments help some kids who have autism, but that the research is still being done, and it's not a sure thing. Jordan said that the bottom line is that anyone who advertises a sure thing cure is wrong. I think that if there was a cure, it would be the top story on CNN every night for a month, so I have doubts. I also think that if someone came up with a cure for autism that was cheap, the people who make lots of money selling drugs to families would figure out a way to keep us from finding out.

I don't really have hobbies like some other people. I like to watch reruns of old TV shows on channel 43. My favorites are police shows like Adam-12 and Dragnet. I also like to watch some shows on PBS.

Nobody knows it, but I have a really good sense of humor. I think lots of things are funny, and I think of lots of funny things to say. I just can't say them. These things make me laugh inside. I don't ever laugh out loud. I would if I could. I smile sometimes.

I guess I do have kind of a hobby—I remember funny and silly things that people say—things that don't make sense at all. I collect them in my memory. My mom calls them "old sayings" and I don't always know what they mean. Jordan told my mom that people who have autism sometimes have a hard time figuring out things that don't mean exactly what they say. She says it's because people who have autism are usually literal and that we're "concrete thinkers." That's one that I collected. When I heard Jordan say that, I thought of a person with a head made out of cement.

Sometimes I hear these sayings for a long time before I figure out what they're supposed to mean. Sometimes when I do figure them out, I think they're just dumb, but sometimes they're funny. My dad used to say it was time to "hit the sack" when he meant that it was time to go to sleep. It took me a long time to figure that one out, and it still doesn't make any sense. When I was little, I used to wonder if my dad had a sack in bed with him. I don't think he did.

Once Jordan almost had a car accident and she told my mom that she escaped "by the skin of her teeth." That one kept me thinking for months. I wondered if her teeth had skin on them that I couldn't see. I watched her mouth for a long time to see. I still don't really understand that one.

I heard my grandma tell my mom that "good things come in small packages," and it made my mom laugh. I know that's true sometimes, but sometimes, really bad things come in small packages too. Like spiders. And, sometimes, good things come in really big packages. I was confused about that one because my grandma was talking about my grandpa when she said it. Then one day a few months later, it came to me. My grandpa is a really short person. When I figured that one out, it made me laugh inside.

I have a lot of these sayings that I've learned. I remember them and keep them in my head. If I could write them down, I would put them in a book.

Sometimes when I smile, my mom thinks it means that I love her. She thinks that, even though I don't talk, I can show that I'm happy. That makes her happy. I'm glad it does. I do love my mom, and sometimes I guess that's why I'm smiling. Sometimes, though, I feel guilty because I know that I'm smiling because I made up a joke or I heard something funny. It's not always because of my mom.

Here's a thing that made me laugh on the inside. Once I was watching PBS on a Sunday morning. Bob Ross was painting and talking about how he paints. Bob Ross has big hair and a beard. I think this show was a rerun because he was wearing clothes that looked different. His shirt had a really big collar and was unbuttoned at the top. Bob Ross always says things that make me smile. He has a very calm voice. He says things like, "Let's just put in some trees. Maybe they live over here." He says, "We don't make mistakes. Just happy little accidents." I love that. He uses the show to teach people to paint the way he does. I don't think many people who watch him can do it the way Bob Ross does, but he always says things about how easy it is. On this Sunday morning, Bob Ross was painting a tree. He said, "I like to think that maybe a rabbit lives near these trees. When I was a little boy, my dad used to tell me the best way to catch a rabbit was to hide behind a tree and make a noise like a carrot." I think that's very funny and I smiled the whole day thinking about it.

I also like boys. No one knows that. I know that my mom thinks I don't have any feelings like that. I heard her tell Jordan that. She said at least she's lucky that I'm not boy crazy like other 17 year old girls. It bothers me that she said that. It was like she was saying, "Well, Anna has lots of problems, and I don't get to do things that I'd like to do, but at least I don't have to worry about sex."

It's true that I don't have sex and that I don't hang out with boys. But I want to. Not the sex part, really, but I want to hang out with boys. Maybe the sex part too. I don't really know enough about it to decide. I only know what I've seen in movies and TV shows. I know that my mom doesn't think about me having feelings like that. Sometimes I don't think she believes I have feelings at all but I know she doesn't think I have feelings about boys. I don't really have a boy in mind. I just like boys. I like to watch them and to think about them. I guess I daydream about them. Just because I can't talk about it doesn't mean it isn't there.

Because I can't talk, I can't tell my mom what clothes I want to buy or what I like to wear. My mom just goes to Wal-Mart and buys things for me. Because she doesn't think of me as caring about boys or about wanting to look nice, she just buys clothes that are easy. Easy to clean, easy to put on and take off, and easy to fold up and put away. I wish I could tell her that I do want to look nice. I would like to look pretty just once. I wish I could tell her that I hate the denim pants with the stretch waist and balloon bottom, and the sweatshirts that I wear over them. I understand why she buys them, but they're ugly. They make me feel ugly too.

I also wish I could wear makeup some times. Not too much. I don't want to be like my dad's new wife. My mom says she looks trashy. At first, I didn't know what that meant. I thought that meant she looked like a garbage can and that made me smile. Then I figured out that it means that my mom thinks she looks naughty. I don't want to be trashy, but I would like to look pretty like my mom. If I could tell my mom how I feel, I'd tell her that I want to shave my legs like she does and maybe paint my nails.

I feel kind of guilty about wanting these things. I know my mom does her best and I know she doesn't know that I have these feelings. I think if I could tell her she'd understand.

Anyway, that's me. I'm Analisse. You can call me Anna. I have autism, and I don't speak. I have a mom who loves me, and tries really hard to make our lives work. I know she's not always happy, and I know that I'm part of the reason. As if these things weren't frustrating and confusing enough, I saw a person get killed. Murdered. Right in front of my eyes.

Chapter 2:
"Anger is a short madness"

It was a Monday. There were only two students in the classroom when it happened. Two of the people in my class were absent that day, and the other two were being tested in another part of the building. We get tested a lot in our class—the school has to do testing to make sure we "belong" in this class. Miss Nancy and Miss Audrey were out of the room too—they were with the students who were being tested. That left only me, Jimmy, and the teacher, Miss Atkins, in the classroom.

So, I was sitting at my table with a coloring book in front of me. Even though I don't learn anything from coloring, I really kind of like it. I'm not really good at it. I don't stay inside the lines very well. It's kind of fun, and it occupies my mind for a good part of the day. Because I like it (or because I'll sit and do it for a long time) the teachers put crayons or markers and a book or a copied worksheet in front of me every day. I spend most of my day like this. Because I'll sit and color in a book for hours, I'm not a problem for the teachers—they call me one of the "easy ones" and they don't worry about keeping me busy. When I'm calm, coloring, I don't make loud sounds, so I don't attract attention from the teachers, and in this class, if you don't act out, you don't get attention.

Jimmy, the other student in the room on that Monday, is not one of the easy ones. He has what the Miss Atkins calls behavior problems. She says that to the principal, Mrs. Riley, and to Jimmy's mom. Miss Atkins talks to Miss Nancy and Miss Audrey all the time about Jimmy. They try lots of things to make him sit still and be quiet. He also is what they call non-verbal like me, although he has some words that he says over and over, and he repeats what other people say. Sometimes he can answer questions. The teachers say that he has "echolalia" when they have meetings with his mom or the speech teacher. He is loud, and he does things that really make adults crazy. The teachers get really frustrated with him all the time, and lots of times, they yell at him. I've even seen Miss Nancy push him down into his chair when they get really mad at him. It seems like it would hurt him, but he never acts like it does. Jimmy does things to help the teachers sometimes too. They ask him to do things for them and he likes to help.

I thought Jimmy did some funny things. He made me laugh inside sometimes. Once Miss Atkins was doing something at her desk and she used up the last page of a notepad. She didn't want to get up from her desk, so she said, "Jimmy, will you see if there's another notepad like this one in the cabinet?" When Jimmy came back and sat down, Miss Atkins said, "Was there another notepad?" Jimmy said, "Yes." Miss Atkins didn't think it was funny, but I did. She didn't ask him to bring her a notepad, she just asked if there was one.

On the day that it happened, Jimmy went to the bathroom (which is part of our classroom so we don't have to leave and go down the hall like the other students) and when he came out, he had a hand full of poop. He does this a lot when he goes to the bathroom by himself. I don't know why he does it—I always think it's just something that he can't control, like my loud sounds. When he came out, he went right up to Miss Atkins and before she could turn away, he smeared the poop on her sweater. She was stapling some papers together. When Jimmy smeared the poop on her sweater, she dropped the papers. Her face changed—she was so angry. Her face got so red I thought her head might explode. Jimmy was just looking at her, smiling. She said, "You goddamned little moron freak—this is a brand new sweater" and before you could even blink an eye, she swung around with the stapler in her hand and hit Jimmy on the side of the head as hard as she could. He dropped to the floor, hitting his head on the edge of Miss Atkins' desk on the way down. For a few seconds, Miss Atkins was still really angry—her face was still red. Then, when Jimmy just kept laying there not moving, it changed. The red all left her face and suddenly there was no color in her face at all. She stooped down and touched the side of Jimmy's neck with her fingers. I think she was seeing if he had a pulse like they do on Law and Order. Her anger was gone. Fear was what I saw in its place.

Miss Atkins ran over and locked the door that led to the hall. She paced around her desk for a few minutes with her hand over her mouth. I thought she was going to cry, but she didn't. It looked like she was trying to think, to come up with a plan. It took her a few minutes to remember that I was in the room. When she looked at me, for just a few seconds, I thought she was scared all over again, just like when she checked for Jimmy's pulse. Then she just smiled a weird kind of smile at me, as if nothing had happened and went back to her planning. She took off her sweater and got a trash bag from the bathroom. She rolled the sweater up into a ball and put it in the bag, and twisted the top of the bag around and around and then tied the twisted part in a knot. She crammed the bag into the bottom of her purse. Then, she got soap and paper towels from the bathroom and cleaned Jimmy's hand over and over, till there wasn't a trace of the poop left, and his hand was really clean. She wiped up the floor with the paper towels and took all of them to the bathroom and threw them in the toilet. I could hear the toilet flush three times, and then she washed her hands and came back into the classroom and unlocked the door.

Miss Atkins called the principal's office from the phone on her desk and told them in a very excited voice that there had been an accident in her room and she needed help. She said, "Jimmy fell and hit his head on the table, and he's not breathing. He had a seizure. We need to call an ambulance."

The next person who came in, though, wasn't the principal. It was my mom—she was just dropping by to see me and to talk with the teacher, which she did all the time. When my mom came in, Miss Atkins started talking really fast, telling my mom her version of what happened. The principal came running in just a few seconds later, followed by the nurse and the school's resource officer. The resource officer is a policeman who stays at the school all day. I think all of the schools have one. Our resource officer is young and we don't see him much in our classroom, but I knew that his name was Officer Morris. The principal, Mrs. Riley, and the nurse, Miss Morgan, hurried over to where Jimmy was laying on the floor. They were just about to bend over Jimmy and start moving him when Officer Morris took out his phone and started taking pictures. He took about 3 or 4 pictures really fast before Mrs. Riley yelled at him to get back so they could help Jimmy. The nurse started breathing into his mouth and pushing on his chest. They stopped doing that when the Emergency Medical Technicians came in. They worked on Jimmy for just a short time before giving up and saying that he was dead. They put him on a stretcher and carried him out of the room.

My mom took me home. She took the rest of the day off work, and we just sat at home. Mom cried, and I wished I could tell her what really happened.

Ch. 3:
"A picture's worth a thousand words"

I stayed home from school on Tuesday and my mom took another day off work. I know it's hard for her to do that—we don't have much money, and mom doesn't get paid for days that she takes off. It's just one more thing that makes her worry, and that makes me worry, and sometimes I have a loud day because of it. Today is double trouble. I'm feeling stress because I'm making my mom miss work, and also because I saw Jimmy get killed and I can't tell anyone what happened.

In the morning, I watched Sesame Street on TV. Some people might think I'm too old to watch Sesame Street. It's a kids' show, but I still like it. Especially on a day like today, it helps calm me down a little. Besides, Sesame Street is how I learned to read. I learned my letters and my numbers, and almost all of that came from watching Sesame Street, so I don't think it's wrong for a 17 year old to watch it sometimes. Now, even though I don't have a way to show it, I can read a lot. I can read some things in the newspaper, and I can read reports that my mom gets about my autism. I can read notes that my teachers send home. No one thinks I can read these things, but I can. If I pick up a paper or move it around on the table to look at it, my mom thinks I'm trying to be like her, that I'm copying what adults do. She thinks it's cute.

When my dad lived with us, he used to make me turn Sesame Street off. He thought it was dumb and annoying, and I guess he thought it made me look dumb if I watched it. My dad left when I was fourteen to live with his girlfriend. I don't really like to think about it much, but I know I'm part of the reason my parents are divorced. They argued a lot about me. My dad thought my mom spent too much time talking to the schools and the therapists, and all of the other people in my life about me. He said, "She's not going to get better. Get used to it and stop dwelling on her. You need to pay attention to me and to us." He always talked about stuff like that in front of me. I didn't blame him then because he didn't think I could understand anything. I did though. I knew.

One time when mom was at the grocery store, he got a call on his cell phone from his girlfriend. They talked about a lot of stuff that was embarrassing. They talked about sex. He told her that he was leaving my mom and that he would tell her that weekend. He did. He left our house two days later, and I felt really bad that I knew about the divorce before my mom did.

When it all happened, my mom talked with Jordan about the divorce. Jordan told her that families with a child who has autism have less chance of staying married than other couples. The divorce rate for everyone is about 40 or 50%. For families that have a child with autism, Jordan said the rate is close to 80%. Knowing that seemed to make my mom feel better somehow—as if it wasn't just because she was a terrible person or a terrible wife. There was this extra thing out there that made it harder for them to stay together, and it was out of her control. For me, though, it just made me feel worse.

This thing with Jimmy getting killed reminds me of that time three years ago—this is the second time in my life that I've known something really important that I needed to tell someone. Just like with my dad's cell phone call, I can't tell anyone.

I remember when my mom was talking with Jordan about the divorce, she said that she'd like to be a fly on the wall to hear what my dad was telling his girlfriend about her. I didn't understand what she meant by that—who would want to be an insect? Now I think I understand. She meant that she'd like to be invisible so she could hear what he said without him knowing she was there. That's what I am. I'm a fly on the wall. Nobody notices me. I hear everything and to almost everyone, I'm invisible. I think if my mom could be invisible for a day, she wouldn't like it so much.

On that Tuesday after the murder (that's what I'm calling it in my head) mom and I had lunch together, but neither of us really ate much—we just picked at our food and looked at the plate. My mom didn't say anything at all during lunch. She usually talks to me a lot. I guess in a way, it's kind of like talking to herself and just including me in the conversation. I never know whether she thinks I can understand or not—sometimes I think she's really sharing stuff with me because deep down, she knows that I'm smart, and other times, I think she's just talking to help herself work through her own thoughts. Either way, I like it, and on that Tuesday, I missed hearing her voice.

While my mom was putting the lunch stuff away, the doorbell rang. It was a man who said his name was Detective Wilson. He wanted to ask mom about what happened with Jimmy. He asked if he could come in, and my mom invited him to sit at the table. She introduced him to me. Actually, she just told him who I was. "That's my daughter, Anna. She has autism and doesn't speak."

That happens a lot. I get the name and the description for new people that my mom meets. Sometimes, I get angry about that. No one says stuff like that about my cousins, or about most kids at my school. "That's my son, Mike. He doesn't have autism and he talks just fine." That thought seems funny to me. It makes me angry, but it also makes me laugh on the inside. Sometimes I think about how I would introduce other people if I could talk. "That's my mom, Jan. Sometimes she stands naked in her room and looks over her shoulder to see if her butt looks big in the mirror." Or, "That's my mom's friend, Jordan. She wears a lot of makeup and worries that she'll never get married." Or, maybe, "That's my dad, Richard. He tries to suck in his stomach when women walk by."

On that Tuesday, I didn't get angry about the introduction though. I was too curious about what was going on with Detective Wilson. My mom made fresh coffee and sat down at the table across from Detective Wilson. He pulled out a small notebook from inside his jacket pocket and got a pen from his shirt. I thought it looked like an episode of Columbo except that Detective Wilson was younger. I thought he was about as old as my mom. Also, he didn't have a big old coat. He had slacks and a jacket and a tie. Mom and Detective Wilson talked for a minute about her job. He wanted to know how far from school she worked, and how often she dropped by the school to visit me. Mom finally asked why he wanted to know those things. Detective Wilson said that he was just curious. Most parents don't come that often, he said. Because my mom dropped in a lot, he thought she might have an opinion about Miss Atkins—did my mom think she was too hard on kids? Did she seem too tough? Did my mom ever see her lose her temper? My mom seemed really surprised by these questions. She said, "I haven't seen her seem angry. Frustrated sometimes, but not really angry." He asked if she usually dropped in without calling first. My mom said that the Monday that Jimmy died was the first time she had ever come by without calling first. She said that she thought it was just the right thing to do to call before she showed up. On that Monday, she was at the cleaners and had left her phone at work. Instead of skipping the visit, she decided it would be okay to drop in just this once.

Detective Wilson asked why she didn't have to check in at the office before going to the classroom. Mom said that she did stop in the office. Because she came so often, they just had her sign in on a clipboard. Then she went by herself to the classroom. The office aides didn't call Miss Atkins to tell her mom was coming—they just waved her on by.

Until that Tuesday with Detective Wilson, I didn't know that my mom had always called before she came. I knew that she sometimes called. I would hear Ms. Atkins talking to Miss Nancy and Miss Audrey sometimes. She would sometimes say that a parent would be coming to visit. Sometimes, she would make them clean up a mess, or start working on a lesson before the parent came.

My mom answered all of Detective Wilson's questions about why she was at the school on that day. Then he asked her if he could talk with me. My mom explained that I couldn't do that. He looked at her like he didn't believe her. He said that I was the only person who was in the room and saw everything that happened. He said that the principal and the teacher both said that I couldn't tell him anything just like my mom said, but that there must be some way for me to tell him what I saw.

This made my mom really curious. She asked why it was so important for him to know what I saw. Wasn't it obvious? Jimmy just fell and hit his head on the desk. Detective Wilson looked down at his shoes. He looked out the window. He looked at me. Then he looked at his little notebook and back at my mom. After a long time, he said, "well it seemed obvious at first. Everything seemed to point to an accidental fall. Then two things happened that changed things. First, Jimmy's mom said that he had never had a seizure before. We checked that out with the nurse, and with Jimmy's regular doctor. They're doing an autopsy, but the Medical Examiner doesn't think he had a seizure. Of course, he could have just fallen without having a seizure—people do that sometimes—but Miss Atkins clearly said that he had a seizure. She's a professional—she's been a teacher in this kind of classroom for fifteen years. She knows what a seizure looks like. The second problem is the pictures. Officer Morris snapped those four pictures with his cell phone before Jimmy's body was moved. Everyone was yelling at him to get out of the way, but those pictures tell a story."

Detective Wilson said that when he looked at the pictures, there were a couple of things that stood out. One was that one of Jimmy's hands was clean. Totally, absolutely clean. Cleaner than any 15 year old boy's hand would normally be. That wouldn't have made an impression except that his other hand was dirty. It was really grimy. Jimmy's hands were usually like that. Detective Wilson showed my mom the pictures. He pointed out another thing—the floor right under the clean hand was also really clean.

There was a circle that was cleaner than the rest of the floor. It looked like someone had cleaned that spot with something and made a clean circle by wiping around and around. I knew that was what had happened.

My mom looked at Detective Wilson like she just couldn't understand it all. She asked him what he thought all of that meant. He said that he didn't know, but that it didn't add up, and until he could explain it, the case wasn't going to be closed. I thought he sounded like a policeman from reruns. Like Joe Friday on channel 43 or something. I liked him.

He snapped his little notebook shut and put it back into his jacket. He stood up to go. As he did, he looked over at me, sitting on the couch, making my sounds, and said, "I still believe you saw something, and I'm not giving up. You and I need to talk." He was smiling at me when he said it, and it made me think that he believed that I could think.

Chapter 4:
"Beauty is in the eye of the beholder"

After two days off, we went back to school on Thursday. My mom was worried about sending me back after our meeting with Detective Wilson. He convinced my mom that it was the right thing to do. He said that everything would be fine, and that he would be close by. I wanted to go back. I was ready.

Thursday started with Miss Atkins talking to us all about what happened. Our parents were invited to come in for the first hour. My mom came in. Two other moms were there. The school counselor came along with two counselors from the mental health center. Miss Atkins cried. She told us all how it was an accident, and that Jimmy was in a better place. Everyone cried. My mom cried. Then the principal talked for a few minutes, and the moms went home. After that, it was just like before Jimmy was murdered, except that we only had five kids in the class instead of six.

For a couple of days, things were really strange. Miss Nancy and Miss Audrey were very quiet, and Miss Atkins was extra nice to everyone. She tried to have lesson plans and to teach us things. Mrs. Riley came into the classroom a couple of times each day. She hadn't ever done that before the murder. On the next Monday things started being more like before. Miss Atkins went back to doing the same things she did before the murder. Miss Nancy did the same thing—she started acting just like before. Miss Nancy and Miss Atkins got together and talked about their friends, the other teachers, and everything except the murder. Miss Audrey seemed different. She stayed away from the other adults and tried to work with us on some of the goals that were in our plans. She seemed sad. I decided again that Miss Audrey was a good witch and Miss Nancy, the one who talked with Miss Atkins all day was a wicked witch.

I knew that I couldn't tell anyone what I knew, so I settled back into my routine of coloring and sitting as quietly as I could. I did one thing different though. I watched Miss Atkins. All the time. I stared at her. I had never liked making eye contact with people before—I had to force myself to look at people. Now, I found it easier to look her directly in the eyes. I could tell that it bothered her and that's why I did it. I guess it made me feel like I had some power over a bad person, and that made it easier for me to look her in the eyes.

She tried to pretend that things were just like before, but they weren't. I heard her talking to Miss Nancy and Miss Audrey about me. She said that she felt like I was watching her—like I blamed her for the "accident". Miss Nancy said she shouldn't worry, because I didn't understand the concept of life and death, and that I couldn't understand anything anyway. She said that Miss Atkins didn't do anything wrong, and that she was just having these feelings because she had been through a traumatic incident and it was like having nightmares. She said that Miss Atkins was imagining things. Miss Audrey didn't seem so sure—she looked at me differently. She didn't say anything to me, but she just seemed different. She watched me watch Miss Atkins.

After a few days of class, with me watching Miss Atkins all the time, everything settled in to a routine. Miss Audrey was now talking with the students and trying to help them with their worksheets. There weren't lesson plans, and Miss Atkins didn't want to talk to Miss Audrey about what she should do with us. Miss Audrey started making up stuff to have us work on—math worksheets, words to learn, stories to listen to—whatever she could bring in to the class. Miss Atkins and Miss Nancy were back to doing just what they did before the murder. They started ignoring Miss Audrey and saying things quietly that we couldn't hear. Sometimes they did that while they looked at her and laughed. They wrote things down in our books that we were supposed to take home to our parents. Those things were lies. They made stuff up so the parents and Principal Riley would think they were working on goals but they didn't do those things.

Even though Miss Atkins and Miss Nancy were being mean to Miss Audrey, I knew that Miss Atkins was worried about me. I still looked at her all the time. As the days passed, Miss Atkins started looking at me more and more, and looking more and more worried. She talked with Miss Nancy about me a lot. She said that she could tell that I was watching her and that I blamed her. It made me feel good to know that she was scared. Miss Nancy kept telling her that I didn't know anything and didn't know anything about death in the first place. She told Miss Atkins that she hadn't done anything wrong and didn't have to worry about me. She walked over to my table and sat down across from me. She took my face in her hands and made me look at her. She said, "Anna, you're ugly and you're stupid. If you don't like it, tell me." I just looked at her, and she turned to Miss Atkins and said, "See. She doesn't understand anything at all. No one would sit and take that if they understood the words."

That seemed to make Miss Atkins feel better. They laughed together and went back to the front of the room. Miss Audrey looked at me. She seemed really sad. She touched my hand. I looked back down at my coloring and didn't even make sounds. I didn't like them saying those things, but I didn't think I was ugly. My mom always says I'm beautiful. And even if I'm not pretty, I know I'm not stupid. I know some things that they don't know and I have a feeling that somehow, it's going to be okay.

Chapter 5:
"The cat's out of the bag"

It was just a week and a half after the murder. On Wednesday, we were in the classroom doing what we always did. Miss Atkins and Miss Nancy were by the front desk, the one that Jimmy hit his head on when he fell. They were just talking to each other, not paying any attention to us. Miss Audrey was sitting across a table from me and two other students. We were listening to a story that she was reading. It was a little kid's story about Pete the Cat and his missing buttons that I had heard lots of times, but I liked it. Pete said, "It's all good" and I always liked it when he said that. I was coloring while she read to us. I was also looking at Miss Atkins like I had been since the murder, and Miss Atkins was trying not to look at me. She was looking kind of bad. My mom said that she looked "haggard" and she felt sorry for her. She thought Miss Atkins was feeling bad about Jimmy. I knew that wasn't the reason she was having a hard time. I knew that she was worried that I would figure out how to tell the truth. I was worried that I wouldn't.

There was a knock on the door. Miss Atkins went to answer the door and Miss Nancy got up and came over to the table where we were sitting. She wanted to make it look like she had been doing something with us like Miss Audrey was doing. It was a lie. It made me angry.

Mrs. Riley came into the room. She was followed by someone that I had never seen before. He was a worried looking little man wearing a bad toupee. He wore one of those ties that cowboys wear. I think it's called a bolo tie. He also had on cowboy boots. He didn't look like a cowboy though. He looked like he wanted to be a cowboy. He looked like he wanted to be somewhere else. Mrs. Riley and the cowboy took Miss Atkins to the front of the room by her desk and started talking with her quietly. Mrs. Riley did most of the talking. She had two pieces of paper in her hand that she unfolded and looked at while she talked. The cowboy just stood beside Mrs. Riley and looked nervous. He never said anything at all. I couldn't hear what they were saying. Miss Atkins kept looking up in our direction. She looked scared, or worried. Then she looked angry. She said some things to Mrs. Riley and the cowboy in an angry voice. I still couldn't hear the words, but I could tell that she was mad. Then Mrs. Riley said something back that sounded angry too, and Miss Atkins looked down at the floor and didn't say anything else. She looked like she might cry.

After about fifteen minutes, Mrs. Riley and the cowboy walked out of the room. Mrs. Riley handed the two pieces of paper to Miss Atkins before she left. When the door closed, Miss Atkins sat down at her desk and looked at the papers for a few minutes. She put her head down in her hands. After a few minutes, Miss Atkins got up and came over to the table where we were sitting. She had the two pieces of paper in her hand. She walked directly to the side of the table where Miss Audrey was sitting and stood in front of her, just looking down at her. Miss Audrey just kept looking down at the worksheet that she had put in front of me after we read the Pete the Cat book. She was coloring with me. I had stopped coloring when Mrs. Riley and the cowboy were talking with Miss Atkins because I wanted to hear them, but Miss Audrey kept looking down and coloring. Miss Atkins just kept standing over her, looking at her. She seemed to be getting angrier and angrier. Finally, Miss Audrey looked up at Miss Atkins. She looked a little scared, but she didn't say a word. Miss Atkins held out the papers and said, "What the hell is this all about?" Miss Audrey didn't answer right away. She just kept looking at Miss Atkins. She looked kind of scared. Somehow, though, she looked like she was determined too. She stood up from the table. Miss Atkins asked again, "Why did you do this?" Miss Nancy looked confused. She stood up and moved over to stand closer to Miss Atkins. She finally asked what was going on. Miss Atkins and Miss Audrey were just standing, staring at each other. Miss Atkins said that Mrs. Riley and the cowboy, who was really not a cowboy but the president of the school board, brought in a letter with complaints about Miss Atkins. The two pages of notes that they handed her were the list of complaints.

Miss Audrey just kept standing in front of Miss Atkins and looking at her. Miss Atkins was getting more and more angry. Her hands were hanging by her side. She squeezed the papers in her fist and just stared ahead. Miss Nancy was confused. She finally asked Miss Atkins what was going on. Miss Atkins just kept staring at Miss Audrey. She said, "Why don't you ask her? She's the troublemaker. She wrote a letter to all of the members of the school board telling them a bunch of lies about me. She didn't sign the letter, but she's the only one who could have sent it. Why didn't you say it to my face if you had something to say, Audrey?"

"They're not lies." Miss Audrey didn't look scared anymore. She looked just as angry as Miss Atkins now. "Everything I said was true and you know it. And I tried to talk to you about these things. I asked you many times for help. I told you that I didn't think we were doing what we needed to do for these kids, and you just brushed me aside. You and your little clone here just made fun of me and kept ignoring the kids. I couldn't take it anymore."

Then Miss Atkins really got mad. I thought she might hit Miss Audrey but she didn't. She finally turned away and walked back to her desk. Miss Nancy still looked like she couldn't believe what was happening. She went over to Miss Atkins' desk and they talked quietly for a few minutes. They kept looking up at Miss Audrey while they talked. Miss Nancy picked up the papers and read them. They talked some more. After a few minutes, they both walked back over to the table. Miss Audrey had gone back to coloring with me on the worksheet. I was watching Miss Atkins, but I kept coloring too. Miss Atkins and Miss Nancy stood by the table for a minute. Miss Audrey just kept looking at the worksheet, not paying attention to them. Finally, Miss Atkins said, in a really soft voice, "Audrey, can we just talk for a minute?" Miss Audrey looked up and said, "Sure."

Still talking really softly, Miss Atkins said, "I have to write an answer to all of these complaints. I have to tell them why someone would think I did these things. Then I have to go to a disciplinary hearing with Principal Riley and some other administrators. Mrs. Riley says that I'll have to go to a school board meeting too."

Miss Nancy was just standing beside Miss Atkins, not talking at all. She looked worried. Miss Atkins stopped talking for a minute. She looked like she was trying to figure out what to say next. Finally, she said, "Audrey, I've been doing this job for fifteen years. I can't afford to not have a job. I can't lose my job." When Miss Atkins said that part, I thought she was going to start crying, but she stopped for a minute and then started again. "Maybe I could have done more. Maybe I didn't follow the plans like I should have, but let's be honest, these kids don't care—they aren't going to do anything when they get out of here anyway. What does it matter? Classes like this are nothing but babysitting services. That's the way it's always been, and that's how it'll always be."

Miss Audrey just kept looking at her. I couldn't tell what she was thinking. She didn't answer so after a few minutes, Miss Atkins started talking again. "I need both of you to stand behind me. I need you to write statements saying that the things we did in this classroom were the right things and that we worked together to do the best we could do for the kids. Nancy is going to do that. I need you to do it too. If you'll do it, I promise you that we'll start doing things the right way for these kids. We'll change everything and do it by the book."

Miss Audrey waited a minute to answer. Then she said, "From the first day that I came in to this class, I asked you why we did things the way we do. Never once did you say that we were doing something because it was the right way. You always said that it didn't matter what we do, that these kids can't learn, and that there's no reason for us to work with them. I kept trying to do something, anything I could figure out on my own, to teach them, and I didn't tell anyone that I thought you weren't working with the students. I decided that I wouldn't tell on you—I wouldn't turn you in, but that I would try to do my best in spite of you. I asked for help from the other teachers here. There are some great teachers, and they gave me lots of advice. I never said anything bad about this class or about you when I talked to them; I just asked for help. When Jimmy died, I just knew that I couldn't go along with things being the same anymore. I thought about all of the times that you said bad things about Jimmy in front of him, and about all of the days that he sat in this room doing nothing. When we came back after Jimmy was gone I tried again to get you to teach me what I needed to do for the kids. I actually thought that even though it was a terrible accident, something good might come from it. I asked about their goals, and I thought you would change. For a couple of days, it seemed like you would be different, but it didn't last. The last straw was when Nancy called Anna ugly and stupid. Then I knew that I had to speak out."

It was the most I had ever heard Miss Audrey say. It was like a speech on television, like she was the governor or something.

Miss Atkins and Miss Nancy were quiet again. They just stood there, looking at Miss Audrey. Then Miss Nancy spoke for the first time. She said, "Well, you can't blame me. I was just doing what I was told. Miss Atkins is in charge, and I just followed orders. You'll tell them that, won't you?"

Miss Atkins looked at Miss Nancy like she couldn't believe what she just heard. She said, "I thought we said we were going to stick together. If we all have the same story, we'll be okay."

Miss Nancy looked sad, but she said, "Well, Audrey's not going to do that is she? If she doesn't go along with you, neither am I."

Miss Audrey looked at Miss Nancy for the first time since the conversation began. It was her turn to look like she couldn't believe what she was hearing. She said, "Nancy, you weren't just doing what you were told. You weren't told to call Anna ugly and stupid. That was your idea. You were happy to be mean and nasty without Miss Atkins leading the way. Whose idea was it to put paper over the glass panels in the door to the hallway? That was you, not Miss Atkins. When I complained, you both stood together."

I remembered when that happened. The door to the hallway is a wooden door. On each side of the door, there are narrow glass panels that go from the bottom of the door almost to the top. Earlier in the year, Miss Nancy had suggested to Miss Atkins that they cover the glass with construction paper so people in the hall couldn't see in. Miss Audrey had tried to talk them out of it, but they did it anyway. I remembered Miss Nancy saying, "What we do in this classroom is our business. We don't need everybody who walks by to see what we're doing."

My mom had seemed a little worried about this when she first saw it, but Miss Atkins told her it was just to keep the students in the classroom from being distracted by people walking by the doorway. That was a lie. It wasn't to help us, it was to keep people from seeing what was going on. My mom believed Miss Atkins and didn't ask about it any more.

Miss Nancy looked worried. Then she said, "Well, if no one knows who sent the letter, I'll just say it was me, and I'll tell them that you did bad things too. Who's going to tell them any different?"

Miss Audrey just smiled a kind of sad smile. "I thought one of you might come up with that" she said. "So, I mailed a signed copy of the same letter that I sent the school board to myself. I haven't opened it, but if you make me do it, I can take it to Mrs. Riley and let her open it. I think that will prove that I'm the one who originally sent the letter."

By this time, Miss Atkins had stopped looking at Miss Nancy and Miss Audrey. She was just looking at me. I was listening to everybody, but I was looking at her. She looked so worried and even scared that I almost felt sorry for her. If I didn't remember how angry she looked when she killed Jimmy, and the name she called him, I might have. I knew that she wasn't feeling stressed because she was sorry that she had hurt Jimmy, or because she had treated all of us like we didn't matter for so long. She was only worried about herself, about her paycheck, and her reputation.

I just kept looking at Miss Atkins. She didn't take her eyes off me for a long time. Miss Nancy finally said, "Why are you looking at her? Are you still worried that she's blaming you? You have bigger problems right now than Anna—you have to think about what you're going to say to Mrs. Riley." I kept looking at Miss Atkins. I thought that she might not have bigger problems than me.

Chapter 6:
“What a teacher writes on the blackboard of life can never be erased”

For the next couple of weeks, we didn’t know what was going on. My mom talked to me about it all the time. As usual, I didn’t know if she was really talking to me or just talking to herself about the investigation. She talked with Jordan about it too. Jordan didn’t know Miss Atkins very well, so she didn’t know whether anything that was in the complaints was true.

A couple of days after Mrs. Riley brought the letter to the classroom, Miss Atkins was suspended. Jordan told my mom that the school board wasn’t going to suspend her till they had the disciplinary hearing, but that someone had told everyone in the school about the complaints, and the gossip was going around the town like wildfire. The school board and the Superintendent told Mrs. Riley that they needed to get Miss Atkins out of the classroom till things could be settled. They wondered who had spread the complaints but I knew that it was Miss Nancy. She was trying to protect herself by telling everyone all of the bad stuff about Miss Atkins. She only wanted to be on Miss Atkins’ side if that would help her. If she thought it would be better for her to say bad things about Miss Atkins, that’s what she would do. I thought it made her look like a terrible person. She was very quick to turn on someone that she had called a friend.

Miss Audrey and Miss Nancy didn’t talk to each other at all after that first day. They barely looked at each other, and didn’t even say good morning. We got a new teacher, a substitute. Her name was Miss Rollins, and she started working hard right away. She studied each student's plan (they're called "IEP's"—that stands for Individual Educational Program) and made up lesson plans for each of us from those goals. I heard her say to Miss Audrey and Miss Nancy that some of the goals in our plans didn't seem logical, but that as a substitute, she would have to follow the plan. For a few days, Miss Nancy tried to work hard and to make Miss Rollins like her. She said things that she thought Miss Rollins would like, and tried to look like she was doing everything she should. What she did was what my mom called "sucking up". I hoped it wouldn't work. Miss Audrey just did everything she could to follow the plans and to follow Miss Rollins' instructions. She seemed really happy to have someone in charge who would answer questions and help her figure out what to do. Miss Nancy looked like this made her mad. She didn't like it when Miss Rollins told Miss Audrey that she was doing a good job. I think the final straw for Miss Nancy was on the second day after Miss Rollins had made up lesson plans for everyone. She had worked with each of the students, one at a time, to get an idea about how they learned and what they liked to do. I was the last one. Miss Rollins sat down across from me and started talking to me about a story. Miss Nancy came over and said, "She's autistic. She can't understand anything you're saying, and she can't talk. It's like she's retarded. She has the mind of a two year old."

Miss Rollins looked really angry when she heard that. She didn't yell at Miss Nancy right then though. She asked her to wait till she was finished with me. She talked with me about the story, and I wished I could talk with her. She had questions. I had answers. I just couldn't give them to her.

When we were finished, Miss Rollins sat down and asked Miss Nancy and Miss Audrey to sit across the table from her. She said, "I don't know if anyone has ever talked to you about how you should talk to and about the students in our class, so I'm not going to be angry about this. I'm just going to tell you what I expect, and how I want you to behave while I'm here. I also know that I'm probably not going to be here permanently, so you may think that you don't have to do things my way. Let me be really clear, though. You do have to do it my way, or you won't be here. I know that as a substitute, I don't get to choose my assistants. I don't get to fire you and have someone replace you. I've been told that in this district, I'm lucky to have para-professionals in my classroom, and that if I can't work with either of you, I'll just have to work without you. I'm okay with that. I'd rather work alone than to work with people who won't do things the right way. So, let me be clear—I can't replace you, but I can tell Mrs. Riley that I don't need you and you'll be gone."

Miss Audrey and Miss Nancy looked like they were listening to every word. Miss Rollins said, "So, here are some rules of behavior in this classroom for as long as I'm here. First, we will be respectful of each other and of every student in this class. We will NOT ever use words like "retarded" ever again. If I hear that word, you will be asked to leave. You will use People First language in this class. If you don't know what that means, it means that you will refer to students and to everyone we discuss who has a disability as a person first, and if we have to discuss the disability, that will come second. In other words, we won't say that Anna is an autistic person. If we have to talk about that, we'll say she is a person who has autism.

Autism is not in her name. It is one of the things that she deals with in her life, but it is not all that she is."

Miss Rollins was on a roll. When she paused, Miss Nancy said, "I don't see why it matters. Why is that so important? Aren't there more important things to think about than how we talk about people?"

"That's a legitimate question, I guess," Miss Rollins said. "Audrey, do you have an opinion?"

Miss Audrey was quiet for just a few seconds, and then answered. "I've been reading about that. I think the idea of using sentences that name the person first and the condition second is just to emphasize that they are people first. If everyone starts to do that, our society will get the idea of disability as a secondary thing, not a person's identity. I've been trying to learn to do it, and it's kind of hard. It seems awkward in conversation sometimes. The reason that I think we should do it, though, is that the idea comes from self-advocacy groups—so people who have disabilities are the ones asking us to do it. I think because of that, it's disrespectful to refuse."

Miss Rollins smiled. "That's why we're going to use People First language in this classroom for as long as I'm here. One other thing—Nancy, I would ask you not to ever think that, just because a person doesn't speak that they don't understand what's going on, and what's being said. We have many, many examples in our business of people who learned how to communicate in some way after years, sometimes decades, of living a non-verbal life. Don't sell Anna short."

Miss Nancy looked puzzled. She looked at Miss Rollins and then at me. Finally, she said, "Are you saying that Anna might understand everything we're saying every day?"

"That's exactly what I'm saying," Miss Rollins said. "She may not understand anything we're talking about, but she may get everything and understand far, far more than it appears."

Miss Nancy thought for a long time. It seemed to me that she was replaying conversations that she had had with Miss Atkins, or just things that she had said when I was in the room. Miss Rollins added, "I'm not just talking about Anna here, either. There may be lots of other people that we come in contact with in our jobs who know what we're saying when we think they can't understand. I would never assume that anyone lacks the ability to understand."

"Well, I don't believe it," Miss Nancy said. "If she understood, there would be some kind of sign, and I've never seen it. She wouldn't just sit there making her noises all day long, and coloring in that book if she could understand. She would have to have some kind of sign that we could recognize."

"Oh, for those people who understand but don't talk, I believe there probably is some kind of sign. I believe you're right on the mark though, when you say that there should be a sign that we could recognize. I think for people who understand but don't talk, there's a sign, but we just haven't recognized it yet. And, don't misunderstand, I'm not saying that Anna definitely understands what we say—I don't know her well enough to say that. What I'm asking you to do is to make the assumption that everyone we have in our classroom can understand everything you say and do. If you do that, you won't ever be disrespectful. One of my best friends in this business once told me that she has learned to always make this assumption—she assumes that everyone is intelligent, capable, and understands, even when it may not seem like it. She says that she believes doing that will keep her from being cast as the bad guy in a novel that will be written someday by a person that nobody believes is hearing and understanding everything that's said. So, my advice to you both is that you work hard to not end up in that novel."

It's hard for me to say how much I loved that speech. To hear someone like Miss Rollins say that I might understand—that's a big thing to me. I heard that part about a sign too—I never thought about that. I don't have any reaction to people when they talk to me, and when I think about it, that does seem strange. Why don't I have something like that? One of my friends from elementary school doesn't talk, but she gets really loud and pounds on desks and tables, and bites herself when she wants to say something. She still can't really talk, but everyone knows that she understands what they're saying because of her reactions. They don't usually understand what she's trying to tell them, but they know from her reactions that she understands. They know she's smart, even if she can't make them understand all the time. I make sounds, and they get louder when I'm anxious, but that's it. There are no different sounds for different feelings. There are no different gestures to indicate any thoughts. If I do have a sign, I don't know what it is.

I don't think Miss Nancy liked Miss Rollins' speech (Miss Rollins called it a training session) as much as I did. She didn't argue, but she didn't look like she believed a word of it. She did look at me differently though. She seemed to be looking into my eyes. I guess she was looking for a sign too. Miss Audrey smiled all the way through the training session. She nodded and looked over at me and the other students when Miss Rollins was talking.

Chapter 7:
"Between a rock and a hard place"

Because Miss Atkins was suspended, we never knew anything about the hearing with Mrs. Riley and the other administrators. We didn't even hear any gossip, which was kind of different. Miss Nancy loved to gossip, so if she knew anything, she would usually talk about it. Miss Rollins didn't allow any talk about people outside of the classroom. She said the classroom was a no-gossip zone. Miss Audrey and Miss Nancy were still not talking much, so it was pretty much all business.

That was a good thing. Miss Rollins was working with every student, and was keeping lots of notes. The notebooks that she sent home with each of us started coming back with some notes from parents. This almost never happened with Miss Atkins, but now there were good notes coming back. They weren't mushy, lovey kinds of notes, but there were messages about things that the parents saw that were new. A couple of them were even like thank-you notes. Miss Rollins would always read those notes aloud and thank the student and Miss Nancy and Miss Audrey for working hard and making progress.

Miss Nancy was doing her best to follow directions and to do what she had to do. She wasn't always good at it. She still slipped up and said bad things to people sometimes, and she didn't seem happy to be with us. I guess I would say that her work was okay, but not great. Miss Audrey seemed excited and happy and was doing really good work with all of us. I liked when she was assigned to work with me. I didn't really like working with Miss Nancy—I always felt like she was trying to figure out if I really did understand. She just didn't seem to be able to believe it.

My mom continued to stop in to the classroom a lot. Miss Rollins always acted happy to see her, and told her that there was no need to call ahead—she was always welcome. My mom told Jordan that she really liked Miss Rollins and that she thought I liked her too. I wondered if my mom knew that I didn't like Miss Atkins, or if she just somehow noticed that I liked Miss Rollins. One thing was obvious. My mom noticed the communication in the notebook from Miss Rollins, and she could see that we were working on goals from my IEP. I heard her tell Jordan that she wasn't sure whether Miss Rollins was better at working on our goals, or just better at communicating with parents. Either way, she liked it a lot.

After Miss Rollins had been our substitute for a few days, we learned that the school board would be hearing Miss Atkins' case. Miss Nancy had all of the details, but Miss Rollins wouldn't let her talk about it much. When I got home, Jordan came over to our house and told my mom all about it. She said that Miss Atkins had met with the administrators and had tried to answer all of the accusations. Jordan thought that they might have let her continue teaching except for Jimmy. The fact that there was a whole list of accusations, even though they were sent in anonymously, seemed more serious because of Jimmy's death. They didn't want it to seem that they weren't taking it really seriously after a child had died. In the end, Jordan said, they decided not to make a decision. They were going to let Miss Atkins make her case to the full school board and they would decide whether to let her continue teaching.

The school board meeting was scheduled for the next Tuesday night, and they expected a big crowd. Miss Atkins would have an attorney with her, and the school board's attorney would be there too. Jordan said that Miss Atkins had contacted parents to ask them to go and speak on her behalf. My mom was really surprised that Miss Atkins hadn't asked her to come. After all, she was in the classroom more often than any of the other parents. I knew why Miss Atkins didn't ask my mom to be on her side. I knew that Miss Atkins was worried about me being there—she knew that if my mom came, she'd bring me, and she didn't want to see me. She was afraid that somehow, I'd figure out how to tell what I knew. I was pretty sure that Miss Nancy had talked to Miss Atkins and that she'd told her what Miss Rollins said about me understanding stuff.

Mom and Jordan planned to go to the meeting together, and I was glad. I knew that that meant I'd be going too. School was kind of hard for the next two days. I was just waiting for Tuesday. Nobody said anything at all about the meeting. I wondered if Miss Audrey and Miss Nancy would come. I didn't really think Miss Rollins would come, but I wasn't sure.

On Tuesday, school seemed really strange. Everyone was quiet. Even the students who were usually loud and hard to keep busy were quiet. That was good, but it made the day seem even longer. Finally, school was out, and my mom picked me up. We hurried home and ate quickly. Jordan came over in time for us to get to the school board meeting early. Jordan said there would be a crowd so we had to be early to get seats. When we got there, there were just a few seats left, and we made our way up close to the front where there were three together. When we moved down the aisle to sit down, we saw that Detective Wilson was sitting there. He smiled and waved us down the aisle to sit by him. My mom was in front, and she held on to my hand. She led us to those seats. I don't think my mom really wanted to sit with Detective Wilson, but there wasn't a place left with three seats together. Mom sat by Detective Wilson, and I sat by her. Jordan sat beside me. My mom introduced Detective Wilson to Jordan. Detective Wilson leaned over my mom to shake Jordan's hand. Then he said "Hi, Anna. Do you remember me?" and held out his hand to shake mine. I don't like to touch people's hands so I usually just look away. For some reason, when Detective Wilson held out his hand, I put mine in his palm. I didn't really shake hands, but I left my hand there for a couple of seconds. Then I pulled it back and looked away. I saw my mom and Jordan look at each other. I knew what they were thinking—that I must really like Detective Wilson.

Detective Wilson smiled at me, and started talking to my mom. He asked her if she had met Miss Rollins, and if she liked her. He asked her if she had ever talked with the para-professionals, and if she thought they were good. My mom said that she really liked Miss Audrey, but that she didn't have an opinion about Miss Nancy because she never seemed to talk with or work with me. My mom told Detective Wilson that whenever she came into the classroom it always seemed like Miss Nancy was just waiting for her to leave, that she was anxious for her to go away.

At six o'clock, the cowboy called the meeting to order. The room was packed, and there were lots of people waiting outside. The cowboy said that there was a full agenda for the board, but that they were going to suspend the rest of the agenda and deal with the suspension of Miss Atkins first.

The cowboy explained that the board members had received an anonymous letter accusing Miss Atkins of some things that were bad for the students. The board felt that they had to investigate those accusations, and to give Miss Atkins a chance to answer them. He said that these things almost never happen, and that when they do, they are usually handled by the principals and superintendents. In this case, they felt that the full board should hear the evidence.

The cowboy asked Miss Atkins to step up to the front of the room. It wasn't set up like a courtroom on Matlock where the witness faces the audience. Miss Atkins came up to the table facing the cowboy. The school board members were sitting in a horseshoe shape with a table at the front, and one down each side. There were 12 of them. When Miss Atkins sat down, another man came and sat beside her. My mom said he was her lawyer. There was a microphone in front of Miss Atkins. The cowboy welcomed Miss Atkins and said some things about giving her a chance to answer the accusations. Then he read the list of accusations. There were about twenty of them. There were dates and times, and names. Miss Atkins just sat there while the cowboy read the full list. When he finished, he asked Miss Atkins if she had any answers, if there were any of the accusations that she would like to explain. Miss Atkins leaned over and whispered to her lawyer, and then he whispered to her. When she leaned in to listen to the lawyer, she ended up facing the wall to her right. My mom, Jordan, Detective Wilson, and I were sitting near the front row on the right side of the room. As Miss Atkins listened to her lawyer, she looked for just a moment, in our direction. I saw her look into my eyes, and I saw the same scared look that she had in the classroom when she looked at me.

Miss Atkins didn't say anything. She looked at her lawyer, and he started talking. "Miss Atkins has been teaching these children for over fifteen years," he said. "She may have done some things that weren't exactly by the book, but she isn't a monster. She has never hurt any child, and she has done the best she could. There is no proof of any of those accusations, and Miss Atkins asks that she be reinstated to her job and paid for the time that she spent on suspension. We believe that she has cause for legal action against the school district if this request isn't honored. If there is no other evidence against Miss Atkins, we ask that this reinstatement be approved immediately, and that her employment be effective on Monday morning."

The cowboy asked Miss Atkins if she had any other information to offer to the school board. Miss Atkins looked at her lawyer again. I saw her look back at me twice when she was talking with her lawyer. She still looked scared when she looked at me. Her lawyer answered for her again. "We ask the school board to hear a statement from Nancy Ogden. Miss Ogden worked in the classroom with Miss Atkins, and she can tell you what kind of teacher Miss Atkins was, what kind of teacher she is." It was the first time I had heard Miss Nancy's last name.

"Miss Ogden, are you present tonight?" The cowboy was looking around the room.

"Yes sir, I'm here." Miss Nancy started walking slowly from the back of the room. Hearing her voice made me anxious. Even though my mom put her hand on my leg and asked me to be quieter, being anxious made me get louder and louder. That made everyone start looking at us. I felt like everyone in the room was staring at me. When Miss Nancy walked toward the table at the front of the room, she had to pass our row. She looked down the aisle and looked right into my eyes. I was trying to be quiet, but as I looked at her, I couldn't do it—I was as loud as when we used to get kicked out of restaurants. Miss Nancy stopped walking to the front of the room and stood at the end of our row. She looked right at me for what seemed like a long time. I made myself look at her. I stared right into her eyes. Miss Nancy looked as worried and scared as Miss Atkins. She stood there looking at me until the cowboy said, "Miss Ogden, will you join us at the table?"

Miss Nancy looked away from us and walked really slowly to the front table. Before she sat down, she looked back at me again. When she sat in front of the microphone, the cowboy introduced her to the rest of the school board. He asked Miss Nancy to tell the board what she knew about Miss Atkins and her teaching skills. Miss Nancy just sat there looking at the cowboy for a long time. I couldn't see her face because she was facing the front of the room. My mom was squeezing my hand. I was making sounds. Miss Atkins' lawyer leaned over and whispered to Miss Nancy. She turned her head to look at him and Miss Atkins. Then she looked back to the front of the room where the school board members were sitting. She turned around in her chair and looked at me. She looked worried. Then she turned back to the cowboy and after a long pause, said, "I tried to be a good assistant. Whatever I did, I did because

Miss Atkins told me to. I saw her do some things that weren't right, and I didn't speak up. I'm sorry. I looked at the list of complaints that Miss Atkins showed me, and they're true. She was not a good teacher."

Miss Atkins and her lawyer looked at each other. They both had strange looks on their faces. Then they looked at Miss Nancy. The lawyer said, "I don't know what Miss Ogden is talking about. This statement isn't even close to what she told Miss Atkins and me. We're both blindsided by this statement. We would ask the board to disregard Miss Ogden's statement."

The cowboy turned to the school board's lawyer. He put his hand over the microphone in front of him and whispered to the lawyer. The lawyer leaned over and whispered in the cowboy's ear. They did this a few more times, and then the cowboy took his hand off the microphone and spoke into it. "If you don't have anything else, Miss Atkins, the school board will now go into executive session to discuss your continued employment. We will be back to report our decision as soon as we have voted."

The board members got up and walked to a door behind the stage. It was very quick. It seemed like no one knew what to do next. Miss Atkins and her lawyer stood up slowly and turned around to walk toward the door that everyone came in. Miss Nancy stood up too. Before Miss Atkins and her lawyer walked out, Miss Nancy and Miss Atkins stood for a minute and looked at each other. Miss Nancy looked really sad. Miss Atkins looked angry. They just looked at each other looking like they wanted to say something, but neither of them spoke. Miss Nancy looked down at the floor, and Miss Atkins and her lawyer walked toward the door. They had to walk down the aisle. The lawyer held Miss Atkins' elbow as they walked. No one in the audience moved. They just watched Miss Atkins and her lawyer walk down the aisle. Everyone turned slowly as Miss Atkins and the lawyer passed the row they were sitting in. When Miss Atkins passed the row that we were all sitting in, she looked over in our direction. She slowed down at the end of the row and looked right at me. I stared back at her. I thought she looked even more scared than before.

Miss Atkins and her lawyer walked down the aisle and out the door. Then Miss Nancy started down the aisle. She stopped at the end of our row too, and looked down the row at me. I stared back. Miss Nancy looked very worried. Finally, she started walking again, and passed through the door and out of the room.

My mom and Jordan looked at each other. Mom turned and looked at Detective Wilson. No one spoke. They just kept looking at each other and not saying anything. By this time, I was quiet. Jordan finally said, "Well, what just happened?"

Detective Wilson said, "I think you just saw Miss Atkins lose her job. Without Miss Ogden's help, she's toast."

My mom said she hated to see Miss Atkins lose everything. I wished I could tell her the whole story. After a long silence, Detective Wilson said, "I'm not sure she's lost everything yet. I think there's more to the story. There may be more to lose."

My mom and Jordan just looked at Detective Wilson like they didn't understand. I thought I knew what he was saying, and I hoped he was right.

The people in the audience were all talking to each other. No one was leaving the room. It seemed to me like it was getting louder by the minute. The noise made it hard for me to be quiet. My mom took my hand and led me out of the room so I wouldn't be so loud in the hearing room. We went to the restroom. It was cool and quiet in there. We could still hear the sounds from the hearing room. I calmed down a lot. Suddenly, it got quieter and we knew that the school board was coming back into the hearing room. My mom took my hand and we started walking back into the room. Before we could get there, people were walking out. We stopped and just waited as the crowd filed out past us. After a while Jordan and Detective Wilson came walking out. They stopped when they got to us. We all stood there just looking at each other till the last few people in the audience left. Then my mom looked at them and asked, "What happened?"

"Well, the school board voted unanimously to terminate Miss Atkins. She didn't come back to hear the decision—I guess it was pretty clear that without Miss Ogden sticking up for her, she didn't have a chance," Detective Wilson said. "The board president just came back out and announced that the board had made the decision to terminate her, and then adjourned the meeting."

I was glad that Miss Atkins wouldn't be teaching any more, but I was worried that this would mean that she wouldn't be caught for killing Jimmy. I didn't know if I'd ever even see her again, and I was sure that if she got away and didn't have to think about it again, she would never tell anyone that she was guilty.

Chapter 8:
"When fortune calls, offer her a chair"

Detective Wilson asked my mom and Jordan if they had time to have a cup of coffee before we went home. Because the hearing was so short, it was earlier than my mom and Jordan thought it would be. My mom looked at me. I could tell that she would like to say yes, but she was worried about me making sounds. She said, "Why don't you two go ahead and Anna and I will go on home. We have work and school tomorrow."

Detective Wilson said, "Oh, no. That won't work. No offense, Miss Montgomery, but the person I really want to spend time with is Anna." He looked at me and smiled. Jordan smiled too. She didn't act like she was upset at all.

My mom looked a little surprised, but she said, "Oh, I don't think we'd better do that. Anna isn't good with crowds, and she's had a busy day. Lots of excitement. I'm afraid she would have a meltdown in a big group."

Detective Wilson didn't stop though. "I keep hearing this 'meltdown' word as I talk to parents and teachers. I don't know why, but that word bothers me. I wonder how Anna feels when she hears people say things like that."

My mom just smiled. She looked a little sad, though. She said, "I still don't think you understand about Anna. She doesn't communicate at all. She doesn't understand. That's why she makes the sounds she makes. She just doesn't understand about people, and when she's in a group, it makes her nervous and frustrated, so she can't control herself. If she could understand us, we could explain things to her and she could control her vocalizations. I know you want to be able to ask Anna what happened that day in the classroom, but it's just not going to happen—she can't understand what you say, and if she did see anything, she doesn't understand what she saw."

It was the first time that I heard my mom say that I didn't understand things. Still, I wasn't sure that she actually believed it. I thought she was just saying it to keep me from being in a group at the coffee shop. I wondered if she was trying to protect me or if she didn't want to be embarrassed by my sounds. I know it makes sense to my mom that I would be quieter when she asks me to if I could understand what she's asking. I do understand, but that doesn't mean that I can control it. I wish I could explain that to her.

I liked that Detective Wilson told my mom that he didn't like the word "meltdown." I didn't like it either. I heard it all the time. Teachers, even the good ones, said it over and over. When a student yelled or turned over a desk, or hit another student—no matter what happened the adults would say that the kid had a meltdown. I think the word isn't bad, but I don't like it because it gets used for everything that happens.

Maybe I also didn't like the word because of the time I saw one of the people in our class get tied down to a board and stuck with needles because he was yelling and crying and cursing Miss Atkins. The nurse was there, and a doctor came in after he was already tied down. They said he was "restrained." They tied him down so tight that he couldn't move. There were straps around his legs and his chest, and his arms were tied to the board by his sides. He could still yell, though, and he kept doing that as loud as he could. When they put the needles in him, he finally stopped saying anything and was carried out of the classroom on the board. Miss Atkins and Mrs. Riley and some other people talked about what happened. Miss Atkins just kept saying that there was nothing else she could do because he had a meltdown. I guess meltdown was just a way to say that a student was doing something that the adults didn't like. It always sounded like a way to make it seem like the kid just went crazy and no one else did anything to cause it, like the student was to blame. I guess that happens sometimes, but I knew that Miss Atkins did some things to make that kid yell and scream. I saw her put her face about an inch from his and yell at him. She took her finger and stuck it into his chest over and over, and just kept walking forward so he had to keep walking backwards. Finally, he started yelling too. That's when it got really bad. I always wondered why no one said that Miss Atkins had a meltdown.

My mom was determined that we should not stop for coffee that night. I had been making lots of sounds in the school board hearing room, so I know she thought I'd be really loud at the coffee shop. She was probably right. Before we went home, Detective Wilson asked my mom if he could come to our house on Saturday. He said that he understood what she was saying about me, but that he just really wanted to talk with my mom and see if there was anything new that he could learn. My mom said that he could come after lunch on Saturday. She asked Jordan if she would come too.

On Wednesday morning, Miss Nancy didn't come to work. Nobody missed her. Miss Rollins didn't talk about the hearing. Miss Audrey just started working and didn't ask any questions. Everything was pretty normal in the classroom. Miss Audrey was reading a story with me and two other kids, and pointing out the words as we read. Miss Rollins was sitting with two students and helping them recognize upper case letters. After lunch, Mrs. Riley came in to the room. She talked with Miss Rollins at the front of the class by Miss Rollins' desk. She didn't talk to Miss Rollins like it was a private conversation. She said, "I know you've heard about the board meeting last night. Miss Atkins won't be returning to the classroom. You've done a really good job here, and if you'll allow me, I want to submit your name to the school board to fill this position permanently."

Miss Audrey was smiling a lot. I thought Miss Rollins would be happy and would say yes right away. There was a long wait. Miss Rollins looked around the room. She looked out the window for a minute. Then she looked back at Mrs. Riley. Mrs. Riley looked surprised that Miss Rollins didn't say yes right away too.

"These are really great kids," Miss Rollins said. "I like working with them. Audrey is an excellent para-professional, and I think she has potential to be a wonderful teacher. We make a good team. I'm encouraging her to enroll in classes this summer to start working on her degree because we need more dedicated teachers like her. I want to continue teaching with these kids and with Audrey, but there are some things that I would want to change. You may not be willing to make changes, and I understand that—if that's the case, then I'll just pass and wait for another substitute assignment."

Mrs. Riley was quiet for a minute. Then she said, "Go ahead, I'm listening."

“I would want to get the kids out of this room more. I want them to be with the other students more often. Right now, they see other kids at lunch time if then, and even then, they all eat together at one table. I really would like to see them have a chance to be a part of this school. For a couple of them, I want to help them join other students in some of the regular classes. Eventually, I’d like to change the whole system, so that Audrey and I act as consultants with other teachers to make it possible for all of the students to be included more. And I want access to some experts who can help Anna figure out how to communicate.”

I didn’t know whether to like this or not. I was sure Mrs. Riley wouldn’t let Miss Rollins change things like that. I thought this would mean that Miss Rollins wouldn’t be back any more. I liked what she said, but I wished she hadn’t said it. I thought they would take her away.

Miss Audrey had stopped working with us and was just looking at Miss Rollins and Mrs. Riley. She wasn’t smiling now. She was just listening. Mrs. Riley waited for a long time. She said, “Some of the other schools in our district have been experimenting with more mainstreaming of kids like these. Mr. Bruner over at Northern High in Evansville has been doing it, and he thinks it’s a good thing. His students are a lot like ours. I wouldn’t agree to do away with the 1:6 classroom, but if we keep the basic structure, I wouldn’t be opposed to making some gradual changes. I won’t go as far as you might like—I’m not sure about the whole “teacher as consultant” idea, but I’ll work with you on some smaller changes. I think you’re wasting your time asking for an expert in communication for Anna, though. I think we’re doing everything we can for her, and she’s just always going to be non-verbal.”

Miss Audrey looked at Miss Rollins. Mrs. Riley was looking at her now too. "I expected that the change in the classroom would be phased in," Miss Rollins said. "I think that's the way it needs to be. I think our parents will need the changes to be gradual, and I think it'll be better for the students, so I'm happy to do those things slowly, as long as you agree that we'll keep moving in that direction."

Once again, Miss Rollins waited a long time to talk. "I don't want to compromise on Anna's evaluation though. You may all be right about her abilities. I don't know. I'm not saying that I know more than anyone else, and I have no evidence right now that she understands what we're saying. What I do know is that I have had an opportunity to meet a person who didn't speak and who was treated badly because of it till she was 43 years old. She was diagnosed as having, in the terminology of the time, 'profound mental retardation' and she spent her days sitting in a day program for people who have developmental disabilities and doing pretty much nothing. When someone helped her figure out how to communicate, in her case, by typing out words one letter at a time with her index finger on a tablet computer, we learned that she was very bright, that she had been hearing and listening to everything that was said for 4 decades. We learned then that she had seen some really bad things in that day program. She had witnessed, and in some cases, experienced, neglect, abuse, and downright fraud. She named names, and I hope she helped clean up the place, but I worry that after she left, they went back to the same old activities, and this was just one of many day programs doing the same kind of work. We just don't value people the way we should in our society, and if you don't speak, most people assume that you don't think. I used to be one of those people, but now, I choose to assume that everyone can think for themselves, and I believe Anna can do that. I may find that I'm wrong, but I can't sit by and let yet another year pass without doing everything possible to find out."

Mrs. Riley finally said that she would let Miss Rollins contact an expert and get an evaluation for me. I wasn't that excited about it. My mom had looked everywhere for answers while I was in elementary and middle school, and nothing ever happened. I just assumed that I wouldn't be able to figure out how to get the words out. I also thought that this would mean more work for me. I would work really hard if I thought it would mean that I could learn to talk. I just didn't think it would work, so I didn't want to work on it.

Mrs. Riley said, "You can bring in one consulting expert. You'll have to have this person approved by me in advance, and I can tell you that money is tight and we aren't breaking the bank to bring him or her in."

Then Mrs. Riley told us that Miss Nancy had taken a sick day, but that she'd be back with us tomorrow. Miss Rollins said, "Oh, yes. That's the other thing that I forgot to mention. I don't want Nancy back with us. Audrey and I are quite content to do this on our own if you don't have a replacement, but she just isn't a good fit for these students."

Mrs. Riley looked at Miss Audrey and asked, "Are you okay with this?"

Miss Audrey didn't say anything, but she nodded her head. She smiled. Mrs. Riley picked up her things and got ready to leave the classroom. "Okay, I'll leave it to the two of you. I can only say that I admire your determination and your desire to make things better. I just hope you won't lose your enthusiasm when everything gets back to normal and the dust settles."

I didn't think that would happen. After Mrs. Riley left the room, Miss Rollins walked over to where we were all sitting. She looked at Miss Audrey and said, "Audrey, we have work to do." Miss Audrey nodded, smiled, and said, "Yes ma'am, we do."

That was the last thing that either of them ever said about it. They just went about their business, and tried to help us learn things.

Chapter 9:
"One does evil enough when one does nothing good"

On Saturday, Jordan came over to our house early and we watched Sesame Street together. She sat by me on the couch and held my hand while my mom made lunch. Mom and Jordan talked about lots of things while mom worked. Jordan said that she heard that Miss Atkins was getting ready to move out of town. She knew that she couldn't get a job teaching in our town, and she was planning to move back to live with her parents in another state. Jordan said she thought it was in Kansas. That made me worry. I was afraid that if she moved away, no one would find out that she killed Jimmy.

Mom asked Jordan if she thought that Miss Rollins and Detective Wilson could be right. Was it possible that I could understand at least some of what was said around me? Jordan said that it was definitely possible. She said that there were lots of instances where people who have autism learn to communicate as adults. The communication isn't usually by talking, although there are some kids who are nonverbal at an early age who begin to speak much later than normal, sometimes around age 8 or so. Jordan told my mom that she knew some people who had learned to communicate as adults. She said that it wouldn't surprise her at all to learn that I could understand everything that was said. My mom looked at me with a strange look on her face. She didn't say anything.

We had lunch with Jordan and after mom cleaned up the kitchen, Detective Wilson came to the door. Mom and Jordan and Detective Wilson were getting ready to sit down at the table when Detective Wilson came over to the couch where I was sitting. He smiled and sat down by me. Detective Wilson said, "Anna, would you like to sit at the table with us? We're going to talk about Miss Atkins and Jimmy. You might want to hear what I've learned since we talked about it last time."

Mom and Jordan were just watching us. It looked like they were waiting for me to say something. When I didn't do anything, mom came over to the couch and took my hand. She led me to the table and I sat in a chair beside her. I was glad. I wanted to be there. I wanted to hear what Detective Wilson had learned. I just wasn't able to make myself respond.

Mom put fresh coffee in front of Detective Wilson and Jordan and got herself a cup. When she sat down, Detective Wilson took out his little notebook from his inside pocket and his pen from his shirt pocket. He opened the notebook and flipped through some of the pages before he said anything.

Detective Wilson told Jordan all of the things that he had told my mom about Miss Atkins and Jimmy. He showed her the pictures that Officer Morris had taken. Jordan and my mom had talked a lot about it, but Jordan hadn't seen the pictures before. Finally, Detective Wilson said, "Okay, I should just say right now that I think Miss Atkins killed Jimmy. I don't think she intended for him to die, but she definitely killed him and then she tried to cover it up. The only witness was Anna. I know that Anna saw what happened. She knows exactly how it happened, and no one else on the planet except Miss Atkins knows."

My mom and Jordan were quiet for a few minutes. Then Jordan asked, "So, if only Anna and Miss Atkins know what happened, how are you going to get to any solution? Are you really depending on Anna to suddenly be able to tell you the story? Even if Anna understands what she hears, and I don't doubt that she does, she can't tell us about it. If she's able to learn to communicate, as Miss Rollins believes, it's going to be a long process. It could take years for her to learn enough to tell a story like this one. By that time, Miss Atkins will be long gone. And, what judge or jury would believe Anna at that point? It would be presented to them as a concocted story that you or someone else fed her."

My mom was nodding her head. She said, "I'm not sure I would want Anna to be put through that anyway. Even if she knows everything that happened, being put on the spot to testify against her teacher would be traumatic. I don't think I could go along with that."

Detective Wilson listened to mom and Jordan. Then he spoke again. "I've talked with Miss Rollins, and I've done my own reading into this whole assistive communication field. There are many options out there, but I agree with Jordan that no matter what method is used, the learning curve is going to be too long to be helpful in this case. Actually, I read about some cases where a person who was nonverbal was allowed access to a communication device or technique and they just started communicating fluently almost immediately. It seems that the words that were impossible to speak just come flowing out when the dam breaks. So, if we knew the exact right method for Anna, it could happen quickly. Even if that's true, though, the evaluation and discovery process that will lead Anna to that right method or device will take some time. So, no, I'm not thinking that I'll wait for Anna to be able to tell us her story. I have another plan."

Jordan and my mom looked at each other and then they both looked back at Detective Wilson. My mom finally asked the question that I was waiting for. "What plan? What are you thinking?"

"Well, I know that Miss Atkins is really bothered by Anna right now. She has told a number of people that she thinks Anna blames her for the accident. She says that she can see it in her eyes, that Anna stares at her. She's really worried about it, and has said that she doesn't want to be around Anna."

This made me feel good. I wanted Miss Atkins to be worried about me.

Detective Wilson kept talking. "Most people feel sorry for Miss Atkins when she says these things. They think that it really was an accident, and that she feels bad about it. They think she just feels guilty about having a student die in her class, and that she's imagining that Anna is blaming her and watching her all the time. I think Anna is watching her. I don't think Miss Atkins is imagining it, I think it's real. And I know it doesn't have anything to do with her feeling guilty about an accident. I don't think she feels guilty at all—I think she's afraid she'll get caught and be punished, but I don't think she gives a damn about Jimmy."

Mom and Jordan looked kind of surprised. My mom said, "Okay, I get what you're saying. I don't know if I think Miss Atkins did this thing or if it was really an accident, but I understand why you think that, and I understand that you want to catch her. What I didn't hear was what this plan of yours is. What are you saying?"

Detective Wilson smiled again. "Here's what I need you to do. I've been meeting with Miss Atkins regularly. I just keep telling her that I need to get the information together to close the case, and because she doesn't want to seem like she's hiding something, she keeps coming back. I want Anna to be there with me when I meet with her. I want to use her fear against her, and if Anna's in the room, it's going to put some pressure on her. The more we can do that, the closer we're going to get to breaking her story down."

Jordan looked like she didn't understand. "What reason can you give her for having Anna in the room when you question her? Won't that seem like you're just harassing her?"

"Well, it might look like that if I just brought Anna in each time," Detective Wilson said. "But the very first person, outside of Miss Atkins and Anna, to arrive on the scene was Anna's mom. Miss Brooks, if you didn't know anything about this, and if I asked you to come to the station for questioning, what would you say?"

"Well, I guess I'd say that I'm a single mom, and I don't have family around to look after Anna, so I can't come in," my mom said.

"Exactly," Detective Wilson was smiling. "And I would say, 'well then, just bring Anna with you. It'll be fine.'"

My mom and Jordan looked at each other. They looked back at Detective Wilson. He was still smiling. He looked like he was proud of his idea.

My mom finally said, "Well, I have some misgivings about this. I don't want Anna to be put in a position where people are looking at her like she's a problem. I know that if she's in a strange place with strange people, and if there's tension between her and Miss Atkins, she'll get louder and louder. I just don't want her to be put on display and made fun of."

I was hoping Jordan and Detective Wilson would change her mind. I knew that mom was right. I would be stressed out, and I would probably make my sounds, but I wanted to be there. I wanted everyone to know what Miss Atkins did, and if I could help Detective Wilson, I wanted to.

Jordan said, "Jan, I totally understand what you're saying, and I wouldn't want Anna to be put on display either, but if Detective Wilson is right, we sure don't want Miss Atkins to get away with it. And, remember, you'll be right there the whole time. I don't think Detective Wilson will let anyone do anything to hurt Anna, and I know you won't. I just think this is a good thing to do. And one more thing; if Anna really does understand everything that's happened and everything that people are saying, then I'm betting that she really wants to do this. She would want to nail Miss Atkins to the wall."

If I could have, I would have shouted "Amen." My mom looked a little worried, but she finally agreed to meeting Detective Wilson at the station on Tuesday after school. I couldn't wait.

Chapter 10:
"Look at what the cat dragged in"

On Tuesday, the school day seemed long. It reminded me of something that I heard Jordan tell my mom once. She said that lots of people who have autism have time perception problems. She said that means that they have problems interpreting the passage of time. It can be a bad thing, because they may take a long time to understand what's being said, or they may take a long time to respond to people even when they do understand. In some cases, it can be helpful. Some people who have autism can focus on a single thing for a long, long time and still be intense about it. This makes them good at some jobs that take a lot of attention and focus. Since I don't respond at all, Jordan thought that I might have time perception problems. She told my mom that this could be a part of the reason that I don't communicate. I liked learning about that, but I know that's not my problem. I understand time. If I could respond, I could respond immediately. I just can't respond for some reason. On this day, because I was waiting to see Detective Wilson at the police station, I felt like the day was very long. Maybe on this one day, I had a time perception problem. The day seemed twice as long as usual.

Miss Rollins and Miss Audrey worked hard with us to help us learn the things that we had in our plans, and I really liked that they were working with us. I still wanted the day to end. I wanted to go to the police station. My mom finally came to pick me up after school and we went to the station. I was anxious, but I was anxious in a good way. The thing that makes me make sounds doesn't know the difference between bad anxious and good anxious. I was making sounds in the car, and I was afraid that my mom was going to turn around and go home. She kept talking to me about being calm. She said that everything would be all right and that I should just try to be quiet and relax. I wanted to be quieter, especially because I didn't want her to take me home, but it was just too hard.

Mom didn't turn around, though. We went to the station. I had never been there. One of the other officers met us and took us into a really small room. It had one metal table and four old metal chairs. There was only one door into the room. There was a mirror on one wall. I knew from watching NCIS that it wasn't a mirror at all. It was a window. People could watch us from another room. The room was so small that it made me feel more anxious. I was trying really hard not to seem frustrated, not to make sounds but the harder I tried, the more I needed to make sounds.

We waited in the room for a few minutes alone. Then Detective Wilson came in with Miss Atkins. When she saw me in the room, she stopped in the doorway. She looked surprised, and for a minute I thought she was going to turn around and leave.

Detective Wilson must have thought that too, because he put his hand on her elbow and moved her into the room. He closed the door and said, "Miss Atkins, I know you know Miss Brooks. Since she was the first person in the classroom after the accident, I needed to get you guys together to just get all of the facts down on paper. Of course, you know Anna. Miss Brooks doesn't have any help with caregiving for Anna, so she had to bring her along. I told her I knew you wouldn't mind."

Miss Atkins smiled just a little bit at my mom and sat down in the chair that Detective Wilson pulled out for her. She was sitting directly across the table from my mom and me. Detective Wilson sat at the end of the table so he could see all of us. Miss Atkins didn't say anything at all. I stared at her. She was looking at me. She was trying not to look at me, but she couldn't help it. She would look down at the table, and then at me. I just kept looking right at her.

Detective Wilson took out his little notebook and flipped through some pages. I was getting used to this. It seemed to me that he used it as a calming thing. It was like he needed to so something to give him time to think about what was coming next. I also thought that he wanted to give me extra time to look at Miss Atkins.

Finally, Detective Wilson said, "Miss Brooks, you said that you came into the classroom that day just to visit, is that right?"

My mom said that it was right. "So, when you walked in, what was the first thing you saw?"

My mom explained again, the whole thing that had happened. She told the story exactly as she had done before, exactly as Detective Wilson had heard it before. I knew that Miss Atkins didn't know that Detective Wilson already knew what my mom would say. She didn't know that he had already talked with her.

While my mom was talking, Miss Atkins kept trying not to look at me. It was bothering her a lot. She would look at me, and then look away really fast. My mom was looking at Detective Wilson while she talked, and Detective Wilson was watching Miss Atkins. He asked more questions of my mom, and she answered them just the same way she did before.

Finally, after a lot of questions and a lot of notes in the little notebook, Detective Wilson turned to Miss Atkins. "Miss Atkins, is that how you remember things happening?"

Miss Atkins jumped when Detective Wilson called her name. She said, "What? What did you ask? I'm sorry, I didn't hear everything that Miss Brooks said. I wasn't listening, I guess."

Detective Wilson just looked at her for a few minutes. It seemed like he was letting it sink in or something. I thought he was making Miss Atkins wait so she would have to think about it some more. Then he retold my mom's story but he made it shorter. He asked my mom a couple of questions while he was telling the story. I kept looking at Miss Atkins all during the story. I was also still making sounds, but I was concentrating on looking in her eyes all through the meeting. She looked like it was hard for her to concentrate. She looked at my mom. She looked at the table. She looked at Detective Wilson. And even though she tried not to, she looked at me.

Just before the meeting was over, Miss Atkins leaned over and took something out of her purse on the floor. When she straightened up, I could see that it was a package of cigarettes. Virginia Slims. She was taking one out of the package when Detective Wilson said, "Miss Atkins, you can't smoke in here. It's not allowed."

"Oh, yes. I knew that," she said. "Sorry." She put the cigarette back into the package and put the package on the table in front of her. For the rest of the meeting, she played with the package, picking it up, turning it over, tapping it on the table. I thought she looked like she really wanted to smoke one.

Finally, Detective Wilson said that we could go. We all got up and started toward the door. Detective Wilson said, "Miss Brooks, can you wait just a minute? I just thought of one more question."

Miss Atkins walked out of the door and my mom and I sat back down. I looked at the clock. We had been in the meeting for an hour and a half.

"Do you still think I'm wrong?" Detective Wilson was sitting across from my mom and me in the chair that Miss Atkins had just left. "Did you watch her today? She was as nervous as I've ever seen anyone be, and this wasn't even a real interrogation. She wasn't nervous about the questioning—I've met with her several times before and she was very calm and collected. She was only nervous because of Anna. I know she killed that kid, and I'm more convinced now than ever."

My mom wasn't as sure. She didn't get to watch Miss Atkins when she was talking because she was looking at Detective Wilson. She said, "Well, of course being around Anna causes her to be nervous, but it could still be because she imagines that Anna is blaming her. That's been her story, and she could still be acting this way because of that."

"Not to this degree," Detective Wilson said. "She might be nervous and anxious, but she was downright frightened today. Scared to death. I saw it in her eyes. She's scared that Anna is going to tell what she saw."

"Now that we know that she's right on the edge of the cliff, the next step is to give her a little nudge." Detective Wilson looked like he was thinking. Sometimes when I was sitting and not making sounds, my mom would say that I looked deep in thought or that I looked like my wheels were turning. That's what I thought about Detective Wilson then. He looked like his wheels were turning.

"What are you going to do?" My mom seemed a little bit worried, but also really interested. "What kind of nudge are you going to give her?"

"I have Miss Ogden coming in this evening. I'm going to plant a seed. I know she talks to Miss Atkins almost every day still, so I'm going to tell her that Jordan and Miss Rollins think they're just about to get Anna to communicate. I've read enough articles lately to make it a convincing story, and I know that Miss Rollins has Miss Ogden thinking that it's possible. I think that might just be the straw that breaks the killer's back." Detective Wilson looked so pleased with his plan that I thought he might start rubbing his hands together and laughing.

As mom and I drove home after our time with Detective Wilson, my mom talked almost the whole time. She seemed to be trying to sort through the stuff we'd just heard and learned. I loved that she was talking to me, even if it was just because I was the only one there. She seemed to be trying to decide whether Miss Atkins was a killer. She would talk about the reasons Miss Atkins seemed guilty, and then say, "But, of course that could just be her anxiety..." or something like that. Even though it was just my mom talking, it was a good conversation.

When my mom picked me up after school the next day, she said that we needed to go back to the police station to see Detective Wilson. He had called her at work, and asked if we could both come by. I wondered what had changed. It had only been one day since we met with Detective Wilson and Miss Atkins.

When we got to the station, we were taken into another room like the first one. It was in another part of the building, but the room was exactly like the first one. We sat at another table. There were four chairs in the room again, just like before. We sat there for a little while before Detective Wilson came in. He had Miss Atkins with him. She looked bad. Her hair looked like it hadn't been combed and she had black streaks running down from her eyes. It looked like she had been crying. I noticed that she was wearing the same clothes that she had on the day before. She came in with her arms crossed in front of her stomach. She was kind of bent over a little.

Miss Atkins sat in the chair that Detective Wilson pulled out for her. It was across from my mom and me just like before. She stared down at the table and wouldn't look up at me or at my mom. Detective Wilson said, "Okay, Miss Atkins, what did you want to talk about?"

I was surprised to hear that Miss Atkins had asked for the meeting. She sat, kind of rocking back and forth in her chair with her arms hugging her stomach. She didn't say anything for a long time. Then she looked up at Detective Wilson. Tears were streaming down her face. She started shaking. Then she pointed her finger at me. "You have to make her stop. I know that she knows. I talked to Nancy last night, and I know you're talking with Anna. Nancy told me about how the teacher and the speech pathologist are helping Anna learn to say things. I know it. You have to make her stop. Please make her stop."

Detective Wilson just looked at Miss Atkins without smiling or making any kind of expression. He said, "Make her stop what, Miss Atkins? What do you want me to make her stop?"

"Make her stop looking at me. She's been looking at me just like that since the day Jimmy died. It's too much. I can't take it anymore. You have to make her stop." Miss Atkins was really shaking now.

Detective Wilson was very calm and quiet. "But Miss Atkins, Anna hasn't told us anything yet. I know that she's working with some new consultants, but I haven't heard that she's been able to communicate anything yet."

Miss Atkins was still shaking and crying. "But Nancy told me what you said. You said that they're working on teaching Anna to type using a stick or a dowel with a rubber thing fastened to the end. She said that the stick helped Anna be able to touch one key at a time, and that she was already starting to use it."

"Well, the consultants are pretty confident that this is going to be a breakthrough, but nothing has happened yet. We're hopeful."

"Don't you see? I can't take it. Look at her. She's staring at me right now. She knows what happened, and she's going to tell everyone. It's not fair. It's not fair. I didn't mean to kill him. He made me do it. He wiped that shit on me, and I just lost it. I hit him in the head before I could stop myself and he fell and hit his head. I didn't mean it." Miss Atkins was sobbing now. She put her head down on the table and kept crying. No one said anything for a few minutes. Then Miss Atkins raised her head up from the table and looked at me. She had stopped crying. She said, "Well, I hope you're happy now you little freak. You've ruined my life. You've ruined me. Jimmy wasn't going to do anything good with his life, just like you aren't going to do anything with yours. It's not fair." As she said this, her voice got louder and louder. At the end, she stood up and leaned over the table toward me. She pounded on the table with her fist two times. Detective Wilson had moved out of his chair and was standing behind her. He took her arms and put them behind her. He took handcuffs out of the holster on his belt and handcuffed Miss Atkins. Another officer, a woman, came in the door and led Miss Atkins out. She was reading Miss Atkins her rights just like they do on CSI.

My mom looked shocked. She looked at me. She looked at Detective Wilson. Finally, she stood up. I could see that her knees were shaking. She said, "Wow. That was amazing. I hate that it happened, but I'm really glad that the truth is out. Detective Wilson, you did a great job. I'm amazed. You're a great detective."

Detective Wilson smiled and said, "You still don't get it do you? It wasn't me. It was Anna. I promise you that if she hadn't made this happen Miss Atkins would be living with her parents by now, and we would never have found out what happened." He looked at me. "Thank you Anna. I will never, never forget you. I hope you'll let me come and visit some time. You're a hero to me."

I thought Detective Wilson was just saying that stuff for my mom to hear, but I liked it. The truth is, I felt kind of like a hero too. It was hard, but I wanted to make sure Miss Atkins didn't hurt anyone else. I wondered if Jimmy knew that she was caught. I hoped so.

Chapter 11:
"The crow may be caged but his thoughts are in the cornfield"

It took about two weeks for Miss Rollins to get everything in order for the consultants to meet with my mom and me about the communication evaluation. It was a strange couple of weeks. Everyone found out about Miss Atkins' confession, but Miss Audrey and Miss Rollins didn't really talk about it at all. The day after Miss Atkins was taken into custody, they mentioned it to each other, but they didn't have a long conversation about it. I think they must have talked about it a lot but just not in the classroom. It was a really big deal at the school. It would be really strange for them not to talk about it. I think that Miss Rollins was just determined to not talk about things like that in front of the students. I think she really believed that we could understand even if we couldn't speak. They may also have thought that I would be bothered by the story, since my mom and I were there when the confession came. I wouldn't have. I liked to remember how it happened. I was proud of it. For whatever reason, though, it wasn't talked about in our class, and because we didn't get to be out of our room with the other students, I didn't really hear anything else about the murder.

What I did hear a lot about was communication. Miss Rollins was determined to get an expert to come in and evaluate me. She was convinced that I understood what was going on around me, and she was determined to figure out how to help me learn to communicate.

I wasn't so sure I wanted to. I didn't know if I wanted to change. I knew it would be hard work to learn a new system, even if Miss Rollins could find one. I thought that, no matter how hard I tried, it might not work. I could see myself working really hard and still not being able to communicate. That would make me feel worse. I would feel like I was a failure.

I had just worked really hard to get Miss Atkins to admit that she killed Jimmy. Detective Wilson said I was a hero. I felt a little like one. Now I was going to start working on something that would be really hard and I might not succeed. It was kind of hard to think about going from being a hero to being a failure. Sometimes I thought I wanted to communicate, and sometimes I just wanted to go on the same way I had always done. At least I knew how to live that way. I had no idea how to live my life if I would be expected to say things.

Besides, I kept wondering if being able to communicate would be such a good thing. What if I could understand what people were saying but didn't have anything important to say? Maybe it would be better to have people think I could think without having to say things that proved it. I just wasn't sure that my life would be better if I could communicate. I had lived 17 years without being able to answer a question or tell people anything, and being able to do that now would be a big change. My whole life would change. Was it worth it? I wasn't sure.

What finally made me want to do it? I decided that I owed it to Jimmy. I owed it to my mom, and to Jordan, and to Miss Rollins, and to Detective Wilson, and to anyone else who believed that I was smart. I also decided that I owed it to myself to be able to speak out. I also wanted to tell my mom "thank you" for sticking with me. I remembered kids that I started school with in kindergarten who weren't around anymore. They didn't go to our school anymore because they were living in an institution somewhere. I had heard my mom and dad talking about institutions before and I had heard teachers talk about some of the kids who weren't in our school any more. They would talk about them being "sent away" to live in an institution.

I knew that when I was younger, my dad wanted my mom to visit an institution. My mom wouldn't do it. She wouldn't talk to him about it. She cried and cried, but she wouldn't let him consider putting me away.

I still didn't know if my mom believed I could understand things. I think she did sometimes and at other times she didn't. Whether she loved me and wanted to make me happy was not a question though. She gave up a lot to keep me at home and to keep us together.

So, when Miss Rollins got the experts from the state university to come to our classroom, I was ready to work with them. There were two people who came. Dr. Whitley was a teacher and a researcher who had worked with lots of communication problems. She was a happy person who smiled a lot. Dr. Langley was an expert on communication devices and computers. I spent lots of time with them. I had an evaluation to make sure there was nothing that would make it physically impossible for me to speak or to communicate. They did evaluations on my motor movements. They talked a lot about fine motor skills and gross motor skills. I tried to do everything they asked me to do. They said that my "case" was really different. "Bewildering" is the word that Dr. Whitley used. I had gross motor movements that were in "acceptable ranges" which is why I can walk. My walking is not totally normal, Dr. Whitley said, but it allows me to be mobile. It seemed to surprise the professors that I had enough motor control to walk and to hold a spoon and eat by myself, but not enough control to point at things when they asked me to. I didn't understand it either. I thought it wasn't about gross motor control at all. I thought I could walk and eat because those things were automatic to me. I didn't have to have my brain tell my foot to move. It just moved without being told. If I was thinking something, or if the professors asked me to pick up something or point at something, my brain had to tell my body to do it. My brain just wouldn't do that. I don't know why.

Dr. Whitley finally put together a plan. She described it to Miss Rollins and my mom. She was going to use some new research about retraining the brain after people have a stroke that helped people learn to do things that they had been able to do before the stroke. She said the study was done at Johns Hopkins University and that it involved "precise, intense retraining to 'rewire' a damaged brain." I didn't understand all of that, but I had heard Jordan talk about Johns Hopkins University. Everyone seemed to be really impressed with the idea. I thought it might just be because Dr. Whitley knew lots of big words and was really excited when she talked about it. She talked with her hands and waved them around a lot.

Dr. Whitley was also going to use "hand-over-hand" prompts to help me learn to point and touch. She said that the therapists would ask me to point at a picture, and then move my hand to that picture. The theory was that doing this over and over would train my brain to associate the movement with the request. Dr. Whitley said that there is a danger in this practice. She said that it could work, but that I could get dependent on the hand-over-hand prompt and then not work without it. The therapists were being trained to fade the prompts to gentler and lighter touch as the brain training started to take hold.

My mom asked Dr. Whitley if this process was like Facilitated Communication. She didn't know much about this form of communication. She had heard about it from Jordan a few years earlier but had decided against having me try it. Dr. Whitley said, "I can understand how you could make a connection to FC, but that's not the direction we're taking." Dr. Whitley explained that Facilitated Communication involves learning to communicate by typing on a keyboard or pointing at letters, images, or other symbols to create messages. FC involves a combination of physical and emotional support for a person who has difficulties with speech and with intentional pointing.

"Although there is a lot of controversy about the validity of FC, I absolutely know that, for some people it works, and works well," Dr. Whitley said. "It's not accepted as a valid method by the American Speech-Hearing-Language Association or the American Psychological Association. They believe that FC can cause more harm than good for some people. The FC detractors believe that the facilitator, who physically supports the arm or hand of the person pointing or typing, is actually the one communicating. They believe that the facilitator is, either consciously or subconsciously, typing the actual messages. They call it pseudo-science and compare it to the use of a Ouija board. People who support FC have studies of their own to bolster their cause. They can cite proven examples of people answering questions through facilitated communication that the facilitator could not possibly have answered on their own."

"I have personally known people who use FC, and for those people, it has been proven to me beyond any doubt," Dr. Whitley said. "For Anna, though, I wanted us to focus on getting to a place where there is no question, and where there isn't a necessity for that kind of well-trained and ever-present support. Many people who use FC are only able to communicate with those facilitators that they have developed a bond with. It's an emotional as well as a physical kind of support, and that's limiting. They are often unable to communicate when their tried and true facilitator isn't present, and that can be really frustrating. If we can make this process work, Anna will be less likely to be tied down to a person, a system, or a place."

My mom was listening closely. When Dr. Whitley finished, she nodded slowly. "That all makes sense to me," she said. "I would have tried FC years ago if there had been someone in the area that I could consult with, but at that time, I could only read about it. No one here was doing it. That kind of underlines what you're saying. If we start using a process that isn't readily supported, we'll probably regret it later."

Dr. Langley said that we needed to get me a tablet computer. She didn't expect that I would start using it immediately, but as soon as the team began to see progress in my pointing and reaching, she would like to start me on that device. My mom asked Dr. Langley if she really thought I could recognize letters. Dr. Langley said that she didn't know yet, but that it didn't matter. She said that I could still point at pictures and symbols to tell people what I needed and what I thought even if I didn't recognize the letters.

The computer would be something that my mom would have to pay for. I could see my mom's reaction to that. I knew we didn't have the money to buy one, and I didn't know how we would do that. I didn't want to make my mom's job any harder than it already was.

My mom talked with Jordan about the plan and Jordan was excited. She had heard of the Johns Hopkins University study and thought it had a chance of working. I was glad Jordan liked the ideas because that made my mom more comfortable with the plan. Mom told Jordan that she didn't know how she would be able to get the tablet. She said that our budget was really tight, and that she just couldn't afford it. Mom said that her boss had been really nice about the time she had to miss because of my evaluations and therapies, but that she hadn't been paid for those days she missed. We were already behind on our bills and she didn't see how she could get anything more.

Jordan looked at my mom with a little smile. "I've said this before, and I'll say it again. You have to ask Richard to help. He's not just some guy off the street. He's Anna's dad. It's time for him to step up and help out with this thing."

My mom looked sad. "You know he hasn't helped at all since he left. I don't think he's doing so well now, so I don't know if he can afford it either. I just hate to ask."

"You shouldn't ask, Jan," Jordan said. "You just need to demand for once. This isn't about you, it's about Anna, and if the consultants say a tablet is what she needs, then the least he can do is to spring for it. Miss Rollins has been amazing in getting the school district to pay for the consultation, so this is really the only cost there is. He needs to do the right thing."

"I'll think about it, Jordan. I know you're right, but I just hate to have to talk to him about it."

I just kept working. The professors and the therapists worked with me to increase my motor movements. They were having me come for a two hour session in the morning, and another in the afternoon. Mostly, the sessions were just the same. The therapist would put two pictures in front of me. They might be a dog and a cat. The therapist would say, "Point to the cat," and then take my hand and move it so that my index finger would point to the cat. In the beginning, they didn't even wait a second to see if I would do it on my own. They would just take my hand and help me point. That was the hand-over-hand prompt that Dr. Whitley had talked about. The idea was that, by making my hand make this movement over and over, I would eventually learn to do it on my own. They asked questions that they knew I could answer if I really was smart. The point was not to get me to answer hard questions. It was to get me to answer any question. I worked hard to do whatever they wanted me to do. I sat for session after session trying to make my hand move to the picture.

Over the next four weeks, I did the same thing. I sat and listened to their questions. Five days a week, four hours per day. I tried to make my brain move my hand. It never happened. I was starting to get worried. I didn't know if this would ever work, but I wanted it to and I thought they would give up on me. Then I heard Dr. Whitley talking to some of the therapists. She met with them just before I started my session. She said, "I know you may not think we're making progress, but please don't give up. We have to keep doing this and we're not even close to giving up. And, even if you don't see progress, I do."

Dr. Whitley looked at me then. "Anna, I know you haven't been able to point to the answer yet, but I can see you trying. You are definitely looking at the picture and I see determination in your eyes. I think we're going to get there. I don't want our therapist to give up, and I don't want you to stop trying. You're working hard—don't stop doing that and we'll make something good happen."

Then Dr. Whitley laughed and looked at all of us. She said, "Of course I'm often accused of seeing progress everywhere I look. I know my reputation. I know that my colleagues say that I'm not always realistic. They think I only see the pros, never the cons. I can live with that. I think we're going to make this thing happen."

I liked hearing that. I promised myself that I would work as hard as Dr. Whitley to learn to communicate. I also thought that if I could learn to point at the answers, my dad might decide to help my mom pay for the tablet computer that I was going to need.

My mom was optimistic. Miss Rollins was excited and just kept telling me that she was proud. Jordan was proud. Dr. Whitley was determined. All I could do was just keep working.

Chapter 12:
"Out of the blue"

Week after week, I went to the therapy sessions. We had been at it for over two months. I hadn't been able to point to anything yet. Dr. Whitley was still confident. My mom was looking more and more worried. Jordan even seemed to be wondering if anything was going to happen. Miss Rollins and Miss Audrey just kept teaching us and working on our goals. The parents of the students in the classroom were coming to the class more often. Miss Rollins was always calling them and sending notes home, asking them to come and see what we were doing. I was still just coloring and sitting in the room most of the time. Miss Audrey would read to me and Miss Rollins talked to me a lot. Miss Rollins said that she knew that I was working very hard for four hours each day with the therapists, and she didn't want to add too much to my schedule in the classroom while that was going on.

I was tired. It may not sound like sitting with the therapists and not answering questions would be hard work, but I tried really hard. I tried to make my brain make my hand move. Sometimes, I almost thought that I was going to make it happen, but I just never did.

My mom was more and more worried about how we were going to get the tablet computer. Dr. Whitley and Dr. Langley asked her about it pretty often. Even though I wasn't ready to use it, Dr. Langley wanted to get it so she could get it ready for the day that we would need it. She said she wanted to "load the programs" on the tablet. I had an idea what that meant from hearing my mom and other people talk about computers, but I wasn't sure. I just knew that my mom was feeling a lot of stress about getting the tablet.

My mom was feeling a lot of stress, but somehow, I was doing better. I wasn't making sounds nearly as much, and when I did, they weren't as loud. Sometimes now, I would hum quietly to hear the soothing sounds inside my head, but I didn't do it so loud that it made other people stare at me. Everyone else noticed it before I did. I heard my mom talking to Miss Rollins about it, and that made me start noticing it too. Mom asked Miss Rollins if she had noticed that the sounds were better, and Miss Rollins said that she and Miss Audrey had talked about it. They were both pleased but they didn't want to talk about it till they were sure it was a long-term pattern.

I was worried when I heard mom talk about it. I thought that maybe I was doing better because I had just forgotten to make sounds. I thought that making me remember it might make me start it again. It didn't. I didn't know how long I had been quieter, because I hadn't realized that it was happening. Now that I knew it, though, I started keeping track.

The next time my mom visited the therapy clinic, she asked Dr. Whitley about the sounds. Dr. Whitley said that it was something that they hadn't counted on, but that she had a theory. "One of the reasons I feel so confident about this therapy is that the level of extraneous vocalizations has decreased. I have no research to back this up, but I'm convinced that the motor training that we're doing is having an impact on the vocalizations. I think that Anna's brain somehow used the vocalizations in two ways. I think that, first, it had become a way to reduce the stress she felt because of her lack of ability to communicate. We've all thought that was the case for a long time. Over time, the vocalizations had become Anna's pacifier, for lack of a better term. The vocalizations were comforting. They soothed her. Second, though, I believe that the vocalizations were directed by her brain as an attempt to communicate. If you think about it, Anna's brain was working to communicate, and it came out as the vocalizations that we've gotten used to. Now, Anna is working hard, trying to get her brain to work in a different way—to move her hand and allow her to communicate by pointing at an answer. I just think that working to get her brain to redirect the concentration of effort from vocalizing to pointing has worked, at least partially. She hasn't gotten to the pointing stage, but she has moved away from the vocalization stage."

I didn't know if that could be true, but I hoped it was. I could tell that my mom was really hoping it was true too. Maybe it was this possibility that made my mom decide to call my dad to ask for help with the tablet.

My dad agreed to come by our house on the weekend. He brought his new wife, Roxanne, and they sat at the kitchen table. I was in the living room sitting on the couch. My mom came to the couch and led me to the table. I sat by my mom across from dad and Roxanne. My mom told my dad all about the therapy plan, and about how Dr. Whitley thought I was making progress. She even laid out some of the materials that we used in the therapy sessions on the table in front of my dad. On the table were two big sheets of paper. They were the size of regular notebook paper. One said "YES" and the other said "NO" is really big bold letters. The words were as big as the sheet of paper. Mom left these papers sitting on the table while she talked. She explained that the hope was that I would be able to communicate at some level.

My dad looked like he didn't believe it at all. He said that it sounded like another of my mom's pipe dreams for me. He said that she had to give up her crazy ideas and get used to the fact that I was never going to be able to think for myself. He said that, if she wasn't going to send me to live in an institution so she could get on with her life, she was just going to keep having these self-serving professor types push their crazy agendas. They weren't thinking about my best interests, he said, they were just thinking about their own research.

My mom looked very sad, but she didn't yell at him. She was very calm and quiet. She just asked him if he would help her get the tablet computer so we could continue the therapy. She said that, if he would help with this one thing, she wouldn't ask for anything else.

Roxanne hadn't said anything before that. When my mom asked for money, though, she spoke up. "I knew she was going to ask for money, Richard. I told you. You should have known. I don't think we should give her anything. Anna will be 18 in just a couple of months anyway, and you're not legally responsible then. Besides, you and I both know that Anna can't understand a damn thing. She's never going to communicate with anyone. She's a retard, and you all know it."

My mom had never said too much about Roxanne before. I knew that she didn't like her. The time that I heard her tell Jordan that she was trashy she said that Roxanne's name made her sound like a stripper. I knew what a stripper was and I thought that was funny. My mom had never really talked to her though.

When Roxanne called me a retard, though, my mom looked like she might hit her. She was furious. Her face was red and she looked like she was about to cry. When she answered, her voice was shaking. "You will never, ever call my daughter a name like that again. Do you understand me?"

My mom stood up with her hands on the table so that she was leaning forward and looking down at Roxanne now. I thought Roxanne was going to say something, but before she could speak, my mom continued. "You will not open your mouth in my house again. I have no interest in what you think about me or about my daughter. I consider you to be a non-entity, a nobody. Your opinion of Anna is of no interest to me, but I will not, ever tolerate that kind of language in my house, or about my daughter again. One more word, and I'll ask you to leave. If you won't leave, I'll call the police. Do you understand me?"

Roxanne started to say something, but my dad stopped her. "Roxie, we don't want to cross a line tonight. I don't want this to end up in court."

My mom sat back down. My dad said, "Jan, I know you're angry because of the divorce, and I know that I haven't met my obligations to Anna. Business hasn't been good, and I just don't have the money to help out. Don't let your feelings about Roxanne or about me cause you to lash out in this way. You and I both know deep down that Anna can't learn. She can't understand. Even if I was doing better, this is nothing but a waste of money. Anna belongs in an institution and you just won't face that fact."

That's when all hell broke loose.

My mom started crying and yelling at my dad, and my dad was yelling and cursing at my mom. Roxanne kept her mouth shut. I think she knew better than to cross my mom again. It got louder and louder and they were both yelling at the same time. They were both standing now, both leaning toward each other across the table. They were pointing their fingers at each other and yelling about things that didn't even have anything to do with me or the tablet computer.

I couldn't take it anymore. I started crying, sobbing, as loudly as I could. I was making more noise than both of them put together. My eyes were closed and tears were running down my face. I noticed that my mom and my dad had both finally stopped yelling. I opened my eyes, still crying and sobbing, and saw that, with my right index finger, I was pounding over and over on the "NO" page. I just kept crying and crying, and pointing and pointing. My finger was hurting from jabbing so hard. I couldn't stop. I couldn't stop crying and I couldn't stop pointing.

My mom was beside me and she sat back down in the chair and put both of her arms around me and hugged me to her. She was crying quietly. I kept sobbing. I knew I was loud, but I couldn't stop. My dad came around the table and pulled his chair beside me on my other side. He leaned his head over on to my shoulder and patted my hair. When I looked down at him, I saw that he was crying too. He wasn't making any sounds, but tears were rolling down his face.

I don't know how long we sat there like that. Finally, Roxanne said, "I don't understand what's such a big deal here. So she cried and pointed to a paper. So what? She's still not any Einstein. This doesn't change anything. We don't have the money for this little toy, and we're not going to pay for anything."

My dad looked at Roxanne and said, "Roxie, you shut the hell up. This does change things. It changes a lot of things. I know you don't understand, and I know you don't like Anna. You don't ever want to be in the same room with her, so I get that. But this thing tonight, this is huge. It's not just the pointing. That's a very big deal, but it's more than that. It's the crying. Anna hasn't cried since she was a baby. I don't remember the last time we saw that, do you Jan? She just stopped crying one day, and that was it. It's one of the reasons that I thought she couldn't understand or learn anything. I guess I didn't want to think that she was smart because it was easier to think about sending her away if she couldn't think or feel. Not crying—that convinced me that she didn't have normal feelings. Now I'm thinking that she knew that her mom and I argued about her all the time. Just about every argument we ever had was about Anna. Jan wanted to do more and more, and I just wanted to give up. I would get angry about the time that Jan spent trying to make Anna's life better. I thought she took time away from us, from me, and gave it to Anna. Now that I've seen this tonight, I'm thinking that Anna stopped crying because she was trying so hard not to be a problem for us. Eventually, I guess not crying just got to be a habit—she just lost the ability to show her feelings in that way. It's strange in a way. I think Anna learned not to cry to keep Jan and me from fighting, and because she didn't cry, I thought she didn't understand or feel like a normal person. I'm convinced tonight. Jan, I'm sorry. Anna,

I'm sorry for everything. You'll have the money for the tablet tomorrow."

Roxanne was angry. She didn't say anything, but she stood up and got her purse and her coat and headed for the door. My dad followed. My mom just sat there hugging me and looking like she'd just seen a miracle. She said, "Holy crap. It's like this just came out of the blue."

Epilogue

I had my eighteenth birthday two months ago on July 18th. Since the meeting with my mom and dad, things are really different. They're not different like a Lifetime TV movie happy ending. My mom and dad didn't get back together or anything. No one fell in love and got married. I didn't magically start talking. I'm still not able to point at answers all the time by myself when I'm asked to. Dr. Whitley says that I'm moving through the plan just as she expected, and we're making good progress. The therapists are doing that fading thing that Dr. Whitley talked about. I can almost do it by myself some times. I have some really good days that have the therapists smiling and giving each other high-fives, and I still have days where I don't really move my hand at all. I don't know why. Dr. Whitley tells me not to worry about it, that it's "perfectly natural" and that as long as I'm progressing, we're going to continue doing what we're doing.

That's one of the things that's different. Dr. Whitley told me not to worry about it. Now, pretty much everyone that I know talks to me. They know I can understand. No one doubts that anymore. They still talk to my mom about me, but more often, they talk to both of us at the same time. I like that.

My dad has started talking to me too. He comes to our house and picks me up sometimes and we go to the park or something. We don't do anything big. He's still scared to take me to a restaurant, but I don't blame him for that. He's been through lots and lots of bad things at restaurants. He's been with me when I was really loud and we were asked to leave. He was really embarrassed by my sounds, and he's not ready to try that again. I'm okay with that. I like just riding in the car with him and going places. He talks to me about lots of stuff. He apologizes all the time for not believing in me. I wish I could tell him to stop doing that. It was good to hear at first. After the one-thousandth time, it gets old.

My dad talks about Roxanne too. He tells me that she's not a bad person, and that he thinks I would like her if I spent some time with her. I don't think so. He says it's probably not going to happen though, because she doesn't want to know me. He says that she resents me, and doesn't like that he's paying attention to me now. My dad just smiled once and said that he guessed it was ironic—that he had resented me taking my mom's attention away from him, and now Roxanne was feeling the same way. He just shook his head and smiled again.

My mom is doing great in her job. She works for a small company that makes windows. She's in charge of invoicing and collecting payments. She jokes with me that she's just a bill collector, but I know it's an important job. When she was having to miss work to deal with the investigation of Miss Atkins, and later to take me to all of my therapy appointments, she thought she was going to get fired. Her boss called her in after work one day just after I had started my therapies with Dr. Whitley. It was before even Dr. Whitley could say that we were making progress. My mom explained that she didn't have any family to help and couldn't come without bringing me along. It seemed like she used that speech a lot.

When we got to the office, my mom was really worried that she was going to lose her job, and she didn't know what we would do. She looked like she was going to start crying, but she didn't. Her boss had us sit down. He introduced himself to me. My mom explained that I had autism and didn't speak. He knew that I had autism, but I don't think he knew that I didn't talk at all till that day.

My mom was really nervous, but her boss seemed really nice. He said, "Jan, you've done a great job for this company. You're the best, most organized person we've ever had in this position, and I don't want to lose you. You've saved the company money, which is exactly the same as making us money. The dollars that we don't lose by being sloppy with our invoicing is as important as the dollars that we earn. You have increased our collections by 6.3% since you came on board, and that's a big thing. I also admire how dedicated you are to Anna. My niece in Alabama has a son who has autism, and I've watched him grow up. He's only 11, but he has some real challenges, and I know how difficult it has been for his family to cope. My niece is a caring and loving parent, and I could see her doing the things that you've done to support her son."

I thought my mom was going to say something, but she just looked at her boss. He said, "All of that being said, I can't have you missing so much work. We have to have you on the job. That's why I've decided to set you up with everything you need to work from home. You'll need to come in to the office at least once a week, but by logging in remotely and using a company phone, you can do almost everything you need to do from home. I've had our IT guys working on it, and the cost is much less than it would cost to lose and replace you."

My mom just looked at him. She didn't say anything for a long time. Finally, the boss said, "Well, will you consider it? I don't want to lose you."

My mom just nodded. I saw that she had tears in her eyes.

On the way home, my mom couldn't stop talking. She was very happy. It made me happy too.

Miss Rollins is coming back to our school when school starts again in a month. She helped my mom get the school to let me come back even though the law only says I have to attend till I'm eighteen. Miss Rollins said that the school would let me attend through age twenty-one if my mom thought I would benefit. I wanted to keep going. Now that I'm almost ready to communicate, even if it's just through pointing, I think I can learn more and more.

Miss Rollins said that two of the kids in her class will be going to a regular class for two class periods each day, and that Miss Audrey was coming back too. Because I'm still doing the therapy with Dr. Whitley, I won't be in any regular classes. The therapy sessions are like my regular classes I guess. I don't mind that at all. Miss Rollins seemed excited about things. That made me excited too.

So, it's not a real movie kind of happy ending, but I don't think real life has many of those. I'm happy. My mom is happy. And, the best part is that it's not an ending at all. I'm just getting started.

30493127R00059

Made in the USA
Charleston, SC
17 June 2014